The Wisdom of Beasts and Boogeymen

Short Stories Written in Rhyme

by

Allen (Pud) Deters

Table of Contents

THE SKY FISH

Unfair are the laws of the Sea!
They favor the Top Fish alone.
Great Spirit never meant that to be,
And He heard the deep oceans
    groan.

'Twas the angry cry of the masses
Relegated to darkness below
While the sunnier Upper Classes
Just laughed at their tale of woe.

Great Spirit put the Top Fish on
    'pause'
While He pondered the Lower
    Classes.
Could their problem be simply
    because
They were born without laughing
    gasses?

Okay, so that's an easy fix.
Great Spirit made the gasses too.
He gave the grumps a cheerful mix
And watched to see what they would
    do.

It happened fast, just take my word.

Their mood warmed up! The gas
    expanded.
The fish ballooned and shot up
    skyward
To the cloud tops where they landed.

But there's a limit to their clowning.
Fish don't breathe well in an air
    mass.
It's pretty much the same as
    drowning.
So were they doomed with all that
    gas?

In those days fish were meek as
    rabbits.
No sins to speak of, no bad habits.
Then thunder boomed! That got
    them started.
To put it mildly, they farted.

That saved the day, one little crime.
So now they do it all the time.
When thunderclaps are really loud
You know there's sky fish in that
    cloud!

NIGHT HAGS

The earth was made in days of yore
From clean stuff in a cloud of dust.
"But just for humans!" sayeth Witchlore.
It was terribly unjust!

The bad stuff was left out in orbit.
But bad stuff has feelings too!
Just think of your own armpit.
So it festered. Resentment grew.

Layer by layer, like hailstones,
Hags took shape in that foul smuttysphere
Some describe them as thirsty dust crones.
They crave moisture – or better yet, beer!

They float down at night like slyboots
With towels to cover their rears
Because the Coven needs substitutes
In case a real witch disappears.

So it starts with pollution up there,
And we care! But do we care enough?
We must clean up and sweeten the air!
But those sky fish will sure make it tough.

WITCH DOCTOR MEDICINE

When his pumpkins awoke on the vine
The Witch Doctor faked innocence.
He pleaded, "It's no fault of mine!
Just a *virus*. We'll put up a fence".

But when they turned carnivorous
And broke loose – he bowed his head.
"May the Jungle Gods deliver us -
It's a *Variant!"* he said.

The peasants had plenty of doubts
But in crisis a Witch Doctor rules
Because peasants are ignorant louts
Which is why they have Witch Doctor schools.

"Yea!" he said, "We must make sacrifice!
Bring all your money to my hut."
And he babbled about a 'fair price'
Til the pumpkins got hold of his butt.

Afterward there were sighs and cheers
And bluebirds filled the skies
But the menfolk grabbed hunting spears
And the ladies made pumpkin pies

COVID DRAGONS

The Covid made dragons wary.
Must they quit eating humans now?
The thought – like the Covid – was scary
Because we are their favorite chow.

"The only hope", said a Wise One
"Is cheap masks and social distance.
No parties, no sports and no fun!
In 2 years we might have resistance".

But the Wise Ones remained unmasked.
They partied and drank their home brew,
And replied, if anyone asked,
"We just make 'em. The rules are for you!"

A Wise One caught hungry old Black Jack
Gobbling an armored knight and his squire.
"Now we'll swab you!" hissed the old quack,
"With a long steel brush and some wire!"

The swab from his nose and his mouth
Was negative, except for chain mail.
So the exam moved down, further south,
To the area under his tail.

The Wise Ones clustered in close
As the aggressive swab was employed
And they shouted (as they pinched their nose)
"It's Positive!" They were overjoyed.

But Black Jack's bug was a hot one.
The Positive gas burned their eyes.
And then it ignited the blowgun.
And that was the end of the Wise.

HORRIBILIS DODO

A hundred thousand years ago
Cavemen of the Paleolithic
Were hunted by *Horribilis Dodo*
Flightless birds once thought to be mythic.

It led to a bloody rivalry
Well-known from dragon lore
Humans were always dragon food, see?
But the birds ate them too – maybe more!

Dragons won out with their flame
And the last Dodos took to the sea.
Man's prospects stayed poor all the same,
But they got rid of *one* enemy.

The Horribilis found an island
A sanctuary on a far shore
They shrunk after a while, and
Weren't so horrible anymore.

Now they're gone. Sailors ate them, mostly.
Starving men called them "finger-licken".
The only ones left are the ghostly.
They all tasted just like chicken.

THE PHOENIX

As the animals, two by two,
Boarded the Ark to be ferried,
Noah's uneasiness quickly grew,
Because none of them were married!

The feeling nagged at him a lot.
Hmm…a crowded Ark…the Ark departs…
What's missing? What had he forgot?
Oops. Chaperones for all those young hearts!

As the rain poured and the Ark floated free
He lined up the pairs, great and small,
And by the rules of a ship at sea
Captain Noah married them all.

But the hot-blooded Phoenix birds,
When he pronounced them 'Birds of a Feather'
Burst into flames at the happy words
And burned up, in spite of the weather.

Two chicks appeared in the still-hot air
When the elephants sprayed down the dregs,
But that's why the Phoenix are so rare:
Married life is too short to hatch eggs.

ALIENS

It happened. Aliens from space
Arrived in Peoria on Southwest
Disguised like the human race.
Planning a world conquest.

In a tour of earthly lands
They had seen obedient fools
Bowing to their ruler's demands
Just like home! Like their alien rules!

Peoria was the last stop
To be sure America too
Was just another lollipop.
But here they saw something new.

Protesters with uncovered faces!
Hey! What about the Covid vapor?
Oh, no! Flouting all social graces
They're using masks for toilet paper!

It seemed comic to aliens, though.
Pretty soon they joined the protesting.
Before long they were shouting, "NO!"
And that had a very nice ring.

They never went home after all.
They just decided to stay.
So starships at their beck and call
Never bombed the USA.

So now you know the story, yah.
And you can never say I'm nuts.
The world was saved in Peoria
By those guys wiping their butts.

SWEET LILY

Sweet Lily, a young dragon wench
Was a bridesmaid, but never a bride,
Which was due to the terrible stench
Of her breath, which she just couldn't hide.

Most dragons burn off the bad smell.
That's what dragons do! So why fight it?
But Lily, an innocent belle
Hated fire and wouldn't ignite it.

That left her hopeless in love
With *Bad Bob*, the boy she adored.
Although she was cute as a dove,
Sweet Lily (phew!) was ignored.

But where there's a will there's a way.
Lily burgled the Royal Salon.
She drank every essence and spray
And gave Bad Bob the *come-on!*

But boys sometimes say the wrong things.
Bob said, "Now you smell like a trollop".
So Lily wound up with both wings
And gave ol' Bob a good wallop.

Then she gritted her teeth and shot sparks
At the boy she had hoped to embrace.
Her breath fired at his remarks,
And she blasted him right in the face!

Love was kindled, although Bob lost his ears.
He fell for her in a heartbeat.
Now they've been married for years.
Romance works. Just apply enough heat!

THE MONKEY KING

There should be a global holiday.
Every flag should be unfurled.
To mark the historic way
Man beat Chimp and saved the world!

Great Spirit set store in the birth
Of the fledgling human race.
But as for inheriting the earth,
He thought we should earn our place.

And mankind did well, I suppose,
At keeping the great beasts in line
Til a genius chimpanzee arose:
The great King 'Chimp-einstein'.

He invented a tool – the termite stick!
And his fame spread far and near.
Then he sharpened it – another smart trick,
And used it for a deadly spear.

He ruled the chimps and all the Wild,
Even learned some human speech.
He challenged the human race and smiled!
That might have been overreach.

Our Hero growled, "Hold my beer",
And the human blood in his marrow
Boiled when Chimp-einstein shook his spear!
So he shot him with a bow and arrow.

He was an unknown Old Testament dude
The way I heard the story told,
And after he settled this little feud
They say his beer was still cold.

1ST LUNAR LANDING

In July 1969
A week before Man's Lunar Landing,
Dragon pups got there, first in line,
And planted a flag that's still standing.

They sneaked up in the dark of the moon,
Circled round to the sunny side,
Left the flag and their mark about noon,
And got home a bit late, bleary-eyed.

The next full moon showed no flag, or scrawl.
But how could that betide?
Mum said they just imagined it all
But it's there – just on the far side.

Their flag might not be found for years
But it never will be too late.
Americans will greet it with cheers!
The message says, "Hi Mom!" and the date.

DRAGONS AND GLOBAL WARMING

Are dragons doomed in our modern day?
Will they be banned and deported?
There are clues in the news, they say.
But they're not being widely reported.

Like this notice a while ago
That Underground Press found informing:
Dragons Guilty! Exile to Follow,
For Causing Global Warming!

Dragons appealed to the World Court,
Earth's ultimate umpire
On grounds that a big dragon snort
Expels *no* Co-2 - only *fire!*

But the dragons were denied landing
When they flew in to contest the deal.
Judges said that showed 'lack of standing',
And denied the whole appeal.

Plaintiffs torched them and *barbecued,*
Which made the World Court pre-exist.
Network news was left to conclude
The conviction was self-dismissed.

GORRAH, THE TROLL KING

King Gorrah, all majesty and might
Ogled the wee pixies before him
From his throne on a cold stalagmite.
In spite of himself he adored them!

That didn't work out so well, long ago
When the Queen of the Pixie Race
Refused to curtsy or bow low
And mooned him right to his face.

But now – *three* cute pixies at once!
Gorrah waved for his macabre band
Determined to make the three runts
Dance on the palm of his hand.

And they did, to a graceful climax.
'Twas a beautiful miniature scene.
Gorrah grinned and began to relax
Then they mooned him, just like their Queen.

Gorrah screamed of a huge reward
As guards flailed and missed with their axes.
It was more than he could afford.
But so what? The King can raise taxes.

WASTE MANAGEMENT

Perhaps the apple was to blame
For humankind's endless woes,
And out of them we could name
One that really assaults the nose!

Waste management! Our garbage dumps.
Avoided by the tourist class
We cover them like we cover our rumps
But it doesn't hold in the gas.

Plus we contribute to our potty chair.
It adds up to tons every day.
And dumpster stink hangs in the air.
There must be a better way!

There is! It's found in dragon lore.
The problem is simple, dude.
Your garbage dump stinks a whole lot more
When you live at the same altitude.

Dragons den high on a mountain cliff
So when their garbage gets the heave-ho
They never sniff another whiff
Because the heap is way down below!

We should bulldoze low-lying towns
In the name of aeration
And rebuild them on higher ground
About 8000 feet elevation.

THE TROLL MOTHER

The Night Hag *Ishi* wandered alone
In search of her worldly niche,
Just a pint-sized, gruff little crone
Who wanted to be a Great Witch.

But the twelve who make up the Coven
Turned down her membership.
"No runts!" laughed that dirty dozen,
"But you might join a comic strip."

Ishi fled to deep cavern halls
By way of mysterious sinkholes,
And there, on the big cavern walls,
She painted an army of trolls.

She sent her boys out to wreak mayhem
On her enemies, far and near.
But that just didn't excite them
Like blondes, brunettes, redheads and beer.

Pixie girls piqued their mood!
Despite faults that are not in dispute:
They are small, sassy, brassy and rude!
But there's no denying they're cute.

LORD ORM

The great octopus, Orm, sprawled at rest
And claimed all the seas for his own
But the Great Spirit wasn't impressed
"You're a slug," He said. "That's well-known."

Orm bestirred then, from taking his ease
And stirred water like never before,
Stretched his arms through all seven seas,
And laid claim from shore to shore.

Orm's arms now steered warm waters north!
Great Spirit dropped his old grudge.
This was great and should stay thus henceforth!
"I like it", He said. "Don't budge!"

The Gulf Stream emerged to melt ice
And allow for new nations. That's fun.
Lands like England appeared. That was nice.
If Orm moves, though, it all gets undone.

That could happen. Lord Orm has an itch
Down low, by the usual crack.
Don't move, Orm! Or the weather might switch
And the polar bears will come back.

THE DRAGON QUEEN

All hail to the Dragon Queen!
Hail to the me/my/mine of the Crown!
Get that right or you'll get the guillotine.
She insists on her personal pronouns.

She changes those/them each day
So when her/she falls out of love
It's a very effective way
To ditch a husband they/them is sick of.

That settles who/what. She makes the laws!
But the beheading always fails.
The husbands survive because
The blade bounces off they/their scales.

The Queen doesn't watch. She loathes messes.
That's for the executioner goon
While her/she/self is trying on dresses
For a new wedding that afternoon.

DRAGON RIDERS

Some dragon art just misleads,
Showing a triumphant armored knight
Flying a submissive dragon steed.
That's just dumb – an impossible sight.

Blink that art out of your eyeball.
Knights do NOT ride dragons like a horse.
No one ever rides dragons at all!
Except for goblins, of course.

They team up to raid a village
And the dragon gets any treasure.
But the goblins unearth and pillage
Every drop of strong 'liquid measure'.

They get drunk and their poor heads throb.
If you know goblins that isn't news.
The dragon doesn't drink on the job
But he takes home the flammable booze.

That's for dragon pups' oral hygiene
Where burning alcohol is required.
They must gargle til their teeth are clean.
After that they can play with the fire.

LITTLE MONSTERS

It's fair that each species has offspring
And the Great Spirit smiles on each child
For the hope of joy that they bring
But some are unspeakably wild.

Take dragons. They'll hatch out two whelps
And just let the naughty things roam
They're delinquent, so nothing much helps
And they're not any better at home.

The same story plays out again and again:
Anger builds in the local saloons.
A drunk mob heads to the dragon's den
With pitchforks and water balloons.

It's time, and the dragon mum knows it
And dragon pop, being no fool,
Grabs a brat under each armpit
And hauls them off to Finishing School.

That's inside a volcanic mountain
Quiet, but still hot down under.
Whelps light up at a lava fountain
And make their own lightning and thunder.

When they finish and graduate
What disasters will they cause?
Remember, they teach them to hate
Any and all human laws.

What hope do we have of stopping 'um?
Take your lucky charms and gamble 'em,
Burgle them eggs from the dragon mum
And take 'em straight home and scramble 'em.

LEPRECHAUNS

Leprechauns, as everyone knows,
Have gold, and it's yours if you find it.
Pots of gold at the end of rainbows!
Looks easy, the way they designed it.

You just need a rainbow-ish shower.
Every year there are one or two.
Then calculate miles-per-hour.
It's gotta be slower than you.

When you find it, the gold starts to fade
If your timing is not ideal,
And you're playing a losing charade.
But if you *touch* it, it stays real!

That's when the leprechaun appears
To fulfill his pledge. You'll be told,
You've outsmarted him. It's all yours!
Unfortunately it's just Fool's Gold.

But don't give up now – gee whiz!
You're halfway there, my friend.
The secret of the rainbow is
The Gold's at the other end.

LITTLE BIGFOOT

His mom swooned at the deformity
And the hairy midwife was hard put
To accept such an enormity:
Small feet on a baby Bigfoot!

But Littlefoot grew up, they say,
Mostly shunned by the Bigfoot Clan,
And since he had men's feet anyway
He decided to be a man.

He found men's pants and slippers to wear,
Took an actual bath one day,
And sold snippets of Bigfoot hair.
But his smell drove the tourists away.

That became the story of his life:
A rank, sweaty smell that girls abhor.
So of course he never found a wife
But there were job offers galore.

There were zoos, sideshows, movies as well.
Then he heard about *linebackers.*
The ad said, 'no matter how bad you smell'
So he played for the Green Bay Packers.

DRAGONS AND THE T-REX

Back in the Jurassic, give or take,
Whenever a dragon met T-Rex,
The Dino must die – or the Firedrake,
Because both of them were apex.

On whom would evolution smile?
If evolution had planners,
Would they reckon T-Rex more worthwhile?
Or go with Dragon's better manners?

One night the old earth did collide
With a meteor in the wee hours
Almost everything was fried.
It wiped out the dinosaurs.

Dragons survived because they can take fire.
That is anatomically correct.
 But they also bump evolution higher
By observing bathroom etiquette:

Whereas T-Rex could not scrub the breach
After a big toilet caper,
Dragons, with clever hands and long reach
Always used toilet paper!

SMOKEY AND THE SECRETARIES

The term 'secretary/assistant'
And our whole modern office setup
Was totally non-existent
Until Smokey the dragon dreamed it up.

Old Smokey held damsels for ransom.
Rich girls – not poor ones – for sure.
They fetched him a fortune and then some,
But he valued the poor girls more.

They were street-smart, which pleased the old brute.
Also thrifty, so Smoky arranged
For the poor girls to count ransom loot,
And he never again was shortchanged.

He made an office just off his den
Where poor girls wrote nice ransom notes.
Smokey scored big time and again.
Became richest of all the cutthroats!

Yet Smokey still wanted more.
But when he cut the poor girls' pay
They found someone else to work for,
And that's how it still works today.

LOCH NESS MONSTER

Whence forth came the sea monster 'Nessie'?
That story is lost to the Ages.
But humans did make her life messy
And someone should fill in those pages.

Her story was idyllic and free
Until the pesky tourist things.
But she didn't mind humanity
Until they bombed her with sonar pings.

There was no safe place in the loch
For a surviving Jurassic waif,
And the bombing went on round the clock.
Sigh…if only she knew she was *safe!*

Girl sea monsters have a serpentine tail
And they *waggle* through the ocean,
So the sonar 'pings' miss, and fail
Just due to this natural motion.

It's been like that through history.
You can frown or you can giggle.
But it's never been a mystery
Most girls do have some wiggle.

THE FEATHERED SERPENT

The Aztecs, according to scribes,
Were nomads in Old Mexico.
One of many wandering tribes.
A vagabond folk. Just so-so.

Then a dragon awoke in the mountains.
The *Feathered Serpent* they revered –
Breathing fire like volcanic fountains.
The omen of their tribe had appeared!

Talks got tricky with that Firedrake,
The most violent of beasts,
But they swayed him with gifts of beefsteak,
And several unpopular priests.

So now, with the dragon's fire,
They conquered a nation, all told,
And the Aztec tribe got the empire
But the dragon hoarded the gold.

They say, no matter how tough you are
There's always tougher roughnecks.
But what in the world was so bizarre
It could beat dragons and Aztecs?

If your booty droops, poor Buttercup,
Suspenders will hold up your buns.
But nothing the Aztecs had held up
Against Spanish crossbows and guns.

HICKEY SPIKES

What's fairest on a dragon demoiselle?
What makes the boys flirty and sassy?
Hickey Spikes! The only part of a Belle
That's prettier than her chassis.

The most popular girls have lots.
That's what dragon culture likes.
But how can little hickey spots
Turn into those beautiful spikes?

The belles start by collecting 'love bites',
From every boy they happen upon.
A juvenile rite and delight.
And the moms are all cheering them on.

Of course hickeys will just fade away
Without TLC, dragons know.
So they put on a public display
Because hickeys need sunshine to grow.

They flaunt and parade when they spike
And they're judged when the spiking is done.
'Cause spike necklaces aren't all alike
And the moms want to know who won.

Human girls could do this if they knew.
They also get smooches and pecks.
We could judge them like dragons do!
But alas, they put on turtlenecks.

OORLOG

The giant tree goblin, Oorlog,
Was known to be a man-eater.
He also ate trees, like all troggs
But he thirsted for something sweeter.

Oorlog was getting past his prime
And he had rheumatiz in his knees
But troggs can live beyond their time
By drinking the sap of young trees.

Tribbits – young trees who are awake,
Who talk and walk freely around –
Get hunted hard, make no mistake.
But it beats being stuck in the ground.

Meanwhile, 'we are what we eat', they say
And troggs eat a lot of wood.
But Oorlog gulped a live beaver one day
And his tummy don't feel so good.

Yay! Tribbits should have a free week!
That's nice, but of course it assumes
They don't have to play hide and seek
With the witches, who want them for brooms.

GASSIUS

An orphan, a young dragon beast,
Was adopted by soldiers of Rome.
He would grow to weigh ten tons at least,
But for now they just took him home.

He belched flammable fumes, but no fire,
And they named him Gassius for that.
But his temper left much to desire,
And they finally got rid of the brat.

The Circus got hold of him later,
A star attraction with tusks like spears!
Chained and teased by a gladiator
To a thunderous echo of cheers.

"Now give him fire!" some idiot barked,
And the Emperor turned up his thumb,
And that's how Gassius got sparked.
Hoo boy, were those Romans dumb!

Gassius ripped loose and arose,
Ablaze in the twilight and gloam!
Then he tested the wind with his nose
And torched the whole city of Rome. (54 A.D.)

VAMPIRES

So where are all the vampires?
Based on their long-life ballyhoo
There should be lots if they don't retire.
So do vampires have troubles too?

Not much. They have devilish powers.
They do need good teeth, however.
They must brush them like we do ours
Or their teeth won't last forever.

Well, they don't. They just file the tips.
But would they see a dentist in need?
If a tooth needed pulling – or chips?
Are there dentists who could do this deed?

Nope. The dental mirrors don't work
On vampires, inside or out.
There's no overcoming this quirk
And it puts their future in doubt.

One day their teeth will be gone
And they'll starve. Vampires are screwed.
They need fangs to draw blood and live on.
The creeps cannot gum their food.

THE WEREWOLF

Meet the snappy werewolf, Dapper Dan.
Strictly non-vegetarian.
Great hair. Great teeth. Great night life too!
Could a full moon do the same to you?

It might if you love the bright moonshine.
It *will* if you bear the werewolf sign.
You need to know, so look for it.
It's under that big part where you sit.

Yes, your butt. Don't faint or swoon!
That's why they call that part your moon.
Just use your mirror in privacy,
And tell the world what you see.

The mark – or no mark – will seal your fate.
When the moon is full and the hour is late,
Will you be joining the Werewolf Clan?
Or just be a snack for Dapper Dan?

TRICK-OR-TREAT

Times have changed some dragon aesthetics
They've gone modern in that regards.
Mums have purses for their cosmetics
Pops have wallets and credit cards.

That's a joke. Dragons aren't civilized!
But they do carry purses or sacks.
That's how they haul loot, and the prized
Maids-for-ransom are slung over their backs.

The sacks are just old bed sheets
Naturally not very clean,
But good enough for trick-or-treats
During Gangster Halloween.

Townsfolk set out any treats they've got
So a trick won't burn down the house -
Some cookies, coins, or (on second thought)
Perhaps an annoying spouse.

Dragons skip the poor folks, so relax!
But they also must skip Castle Royale.
If they show up *there* with their sacks
Their treat will be boiling oil.

PILOT LIGHTS

Most dragons spark up their fire.
They should all do that, by rights.
But some ignitions go haywire.
Young Tori had pilot lights.

Nervous boys called it *pilot disease,*
And gossiped within earshot.
Dragon schools do award Celsius Degrees,
But this wench was just *too* hot.

If she barely breathed, she shot flame.
A cough or sneeze sent a fire bomb.
She could randomly burn or maim!
So she had no date for the Prom.

Well, dragons have mercy. It's a fact.
Even when they burn cities they're nice,
Leaving drugstores and clinics intact.
So that's where she went for advice.

Shyly she described her disease:
"It just burns, and it's worse when I sneeze".
It sounded like a job for some lube.
She got Preparation-H, squeeze tube.

As advertised, it put the fire out.
Tori was the Belle of the Ball.
She arrived with five boys, about,
And ended up with them all.

UNICORNS

The young human race, long ago,
Shared the earth with two clashing forces:
Fire-breathing dragons aglow
Versus pretty unicorn horses.

Humans fled to the unicorn zone,
By far the prettier land.
But dragons wouldn't leave them alone
And they were getting the upper hand.

We were dragon food then,
But when the slaughter reached its height
Unicorns, more friendly to men
Intervened and took up our fight.

That fight showed why unicorns were born.
It was not one of history's farces.
They know what to do with their horn!
They stab dragons right in their arses.

The battle was fought in the sky
Amid nightmarish smoke and noise.
The unicorns won, which is why
We have all these unicorn toys.

MIRRORS

Did you know dragons are paranoid?
Over something rather bizarre:
Dragon ladies want mirrors destroyed
For not showing how pretty they are.

It's been that way forever
Since the very first dragon lass
Did not like herself whatsoever
In an obsidian looking glass.

But why? Boys have never understood.
Pretty human girls are often that way.
But if they're fishing for compliments, Dude,
It's best to watch what you say.

The boys care less about their reflection.
They don't mind looking somewhat beastly.
But since girls have this objection,
They smash every mirror they see.

One mustn't be superstitious
But superstition couldn't be clearer:
Even for beasts that vicious
It's bad luck to break a mirror.

Just think if they'd had rear-view ones
In the battle with the unicorns.
They could've protected their buns
From unexpected unicorn horns!

THE NORTH WIND

The Great Spirit, in days of yore
When all Four Winds were hot,
Cooled down the North Wind some more
So today that's what we've got.

It's a climate we can believe in
In spite of the hot air in summer
Because winter makes it even.
But we need snow – or it's a bummer.

Snow is earth's pain reliever
It's like a benevolent beast
It's like aspirin for summer's fever
So earth's temperature is decreased.

The lovely snow reflects the heat,
So wherever it falls, let it be.
Don't shovel your walk! Don't plow the street!
Or earth will warm up one degree.

And when you're done not doing that
Don't let your neighbor do it either.
Then turn down his thermostat.
Let's give Mother Earth a breather!

Simple cell phone calculations,
If we add a lot of zeroes,
Will show these personal donations,
And we'll all be climate heroes!

FUMOMOTO

Fumomoto, the dragon fighting champ,
Who shot fire out his arrears,
And yet lost to a unicorn scamp,
Was a hero in earlier years.

Even he found some things scary
Like Medusa, with her deadly stare.
Her beauty was legendary
But she had those snakes in her hair.

The Dragon King swallowed her lover
And when she appeared at his throne
He laughed and spat the bones at her.
So she turned him into stone.

All who looked shared the same fate -
All the bullies and bums of the Court!
Then she stormed out the castle gate
To stone some more dragons for sport.

Fumomoto, just there, avoided her stare,
Very lucky for the dragon race!
Then he shot a flare from his derriere
And gasified her pretty face.

Working dragons praised him with glory.
They were rid of the bums of the Crown!
So it wound up a happy story
And their taxes went way down.

ATLANTIS

An upheaval, way prehistoric,
Lifted up a new land from the sea.
At least in the folkloric
That's how Atlantis came to be.

Beings from the earth's molten pyre
Beholden to none but their own
Were also brought up from that fire.
From old tales that much is known.

These supernatural creatures
Messed with our natural birth
Giving beasts each other's features.
Thus monsters appeared on earth.

Griffin, Harpy, and Manticore
To name three. There were others.
Earth had Unnaturals before
But not freakish cousins or brothers.

It looked bad for Natural folk.
The Supernaturals seemed like gods.
Any hope for the average bloke
Faced astronomical odds.

But Atlantis is gone, thankfully.
So here is the epilog:
The pagan gods drowned in the sea.
Always bet on the underdog!

GATORS AND CROCS

In creating gators and crocodiles
Great Spirit was typically wise.
He gave them both enormous smiles
But with jaws of a different size.

 Okay, it wasn't really a smile.
But with the huge maw they could choose
Prey of their favorite shape or style
Anywhere in their rivers or slews.

Although He has told them to quit
They find humans the easiest prey.
Both of the species do it
In their own sustainable way.

Crocs like us tall and skinny
With gators, the fats are preferred.
It's just mouth shape, there's no ignominy
In how to manage the human herd.

They're called 'threatened' now, poor reptiles.
That's the dumbest thing I've heard.
Local boys who know their lifestyles
Will tell you *we're* the 'endangered'.

THE MAGIC WEASEL

Covid brought us the Weasel Wiz.
He was on every TV show,
The biggest Covid trickster in show biz.
It was political magic, though.

He promised with a weasel wink
An amazing demonstration:
With magic words (from Marx, I think)
He would disappear the nation!

This was official, so there would be
A tax surcharge instead of tickets,
With partial refunds maybe,
But the refunds would be crickets.

He played it live in a great hall.
At midnight he muttered the words.
Something fell, but it wasn't a ball -
Just a mandate for the common turds.

He announced, as he stalked the aisles,
"For two weeks you must wear masks!
Pinch your noses! Cover your smiles!
That's all the government asks".

Faceless, we disappeared, true to his words.
Years later, that's still where we are.
But just wait til enough of us turds
Get ahold of some feathers and tar.

Galactic Dragons

From the Draco Constellation
An old dragon stomping ground
The beasts spread all over creation
To cause trouble and bum around.

How does that work, you might ask?
With no space ships like the human race?
Silly human! It's no great task.
Dragons like it out in space.

As dragon physiology goes
They breathe oxygen and (equally well)
The dark matter of the cosmos.
So that's it, in a nutshell.

They're well-tuned to the dark matter stuff
They can feel it on their wings
And if they grunt hard enough
They break dark wind, and it sings!

Most dragons ended up on earth,
Fabled land of gold and jewels
But digging's more work than it's worth
So they made up pirate rules.

They were the first Buccaneers
And enjoyed a rich heyday!
It lasted for thousands of years.
But what would they do today?

Well, they'd better not hit Fort Knox -
Home of the Gold Reserve Fund -
Because if they melted those locks
They would find themselves outgunned.

THE BANSHEE

Are you a Royal, or a peasant?
A pauper or a Lord/Lady?
Royals are very unpleasant
And they're doomed to hear the Banshee.

She was an abused pauper in history,
Scorned as a servant lass.
So it shouldn't be any mystery
That she haunts the Ruling Class.

She wails at the rich and famous
Like a ghostly catamount.
But common folk are held blameless
If they don't have a big bank account.

So … how big is your IRA?
Would she think it's a fortune?
If you can't explain it away,
Identify as a street urchin!

Or get a restraining order
By claiming a different gender!
Get her wailing on a recorder,
And demand a public defender!

Today we would settle this in court.
A judge would put her in handcuffs.
Even ghosts should be liable for tort!
Just be sure everyone has earmuffs.

snow giants

They are the OHOLLEHELLOHO
Who don't know which way they're going.
Giant snowmen with giant gusto.
But only until it quits snowing.

Cavemen considered them good luck
They give the dark spirits headaches
By singing and running amok
Until they explode into snowflakes.

Cave moms sent their kids out in furs
To make snow giant scarecrows.
Today, you should send out yours
To do the same thing when it snows.

Give the snowmen great big eyes
And a happy, cheerful mien,
Because goblins avoid cheerful guys,
And they totally hate being seen.

There! You're safe for the winter season.
Dark spirits will leave you alone
So long as your snowman's freezin'.
After that you're on your own.

THE GRIFFIN

A lion pop? An eagle mum?
That's an interesting blend.
The egg is warmed by the desert sun
Til a beak breaks out the end.

No big deal. This isn't sex ed.
That's just where griffins come from.
But what if the chick has a lion's head
With the eagle wings and bum?

Happened once, looking back in hind sight.
A very odd chick to look at:
The head had too much appetite
And the eagle chick got fat.

The creature got too fat to walk
And waddled into the sea.
It sank with a final squawk
And the heinie bobbed up for all to see.

A boy thought it was a whale out there
And shared this in school, never doubting,
How the great whale came up for air
With the noisy blowhole spouting.

JACKALOPE

Cowboy boots stomp rattlesnakes.
Cowboy hats block the hot sun.
Cowboys just laugh at earthquakes.
But for Jackalope they pack a gun.

Feared throughout the Cowboy West
Are the *Terribilis Jackalopes.*
Notorious, but rare at best
Because young jackalopes are dopes.

Bad temper is their birthright
Which spells trouble for a pup.
They dare big predators to fight
So most are eaten up.

Still, they rule the Great Plains at high noon
But they have a curious quirk:
They get spellbound by the moon.
Very odd for a beast so berserk.

Though stiff as stone, as if they're stuffed,
They're just hypnotized that way.
That's when they should be hog-tied and cuffed!
But folks put them on display.

Try snapping your fingers at one's nose.
Fingers will tell if he's awake.
And if you still have five of those,
Your jackalope is a fake.

ORIENTAL WATER DRAGONS

Water dragons were common in China
When the fire-breathers arrived.
But with no wings or fire, their luck kinda
Took a hit. Let's say it nosedived.

They had been historically present
In that land, stalking about,
Gobbling every stray peasant.
Now they were down – but not out!

They made a truce with the Chinese,
Joining forces with a common desire,
And using all their expertise
They invented exploding fire!

That saved the whole Tang Dynasty
But water dragons got shot at too,
So they fled to the South China Sea
To become sea serpents! Who knew?

Sea life has not been as pleasant.
The water dragon's favorite dish
Used to be hot, charbroiled peasant.
Now they subsist on cold fish.

CHIMNEY SWEEPS

Today, with our clean-burning fuel,
Chimneys hardly get dirty at all.
Chimney Sweeps have no work, as a rule.
But at least the dragons still call.

They have that explosive body type
And blast fire, unlike other folks.
But their throat is sort of a stove pipe.
It always smolders and smokes.

Soot builds up in there until
Dragons must clean out the debris.
Only Chimney Sweeps have such skill
And they charge exorbitant fees.

Can't blame 'em, it's very risky.
The danger is plain to see.
Some dragons, with too much whiskey,
Eat the Sweeper so the job is free.

Nowadays, pre-pay is built in
And the fee is held in escrow
So the Chimney Sweep's next of kin
Will at least end up with the dough.

And they will not estimate a cost
For a related job that's such a bummer.
You know – their lower exhaust.
That tubing can wait for a plumber.

DOG LEASHES

Do you have an adorable pup
Who acts a bit scatterbrained?
Won't learn? His mind seems made up?
Well, surprise! *You're* the one being trained.

No offense, but a normal Yuppie
Who visits a Puppy Show Room,
Will purchase (besides a puppy)
Their own personal leash of doom.

Those are doom for the whole Human Race!
Don't you see the loops on both ends?
You are blind to what's taking place.
And so are your city friends.

Whenever the dogs stop to pee,
Which humans insanely condone,
They are marking their territory.
They are claiming the world for their own!

It's too late for humans to quit.
Soon all that's left will be Old Trappers
Who are wise to doggie secrets and sit
With their coffee, on their crappers.

Can they still save us? Where is one?
Yes they can. I know one. It's me!
I've drank 3 cups now, and gotta run.
I'm off to mark my territory!

THE 'GATTO' AND THE GOLDFISH

The cat eyed the fish with a wish.
'Seafood is me-food' was his motto.
"Gattos can't swim", laughed the goldfish,
"So don't threaten me, stupid Gatto!"

In moments the fish was cat chow
Yeah, so sad. But the bigger shame
Was that water splashed onto a cow
Who kicked a lamp with an open flame.

It was Mrs. O'Leary's milk cow,
And the consequences were dire.
So that's the whole story now
Of the Great Chicago Fire.

This news should be well-received
By the Irish, who were blamed.
For a hundred years they've been peeved.
And now we know they were framed.

Three of the four guilty perps
Actually weren't even Irish!
And the worst of the guilty twerps
Was a cheap Italian goldfish.

FRANKENSTEIN REBOOT

It wasn't supposed to be this way.
Frankenstein was just two weeks old
When he fell apart in disarray.
The stitches didn't hold.

The good doctor hauled him in 3 carts
To 'Good Witches Hems and Stitches',
Modestly tucking the underparts
Into Frankenstein's own britches.

Cheerful ladies in their black hats
With clothespins on every hook nose
Put icky parts in formaldehyde vats
And began stitching thumbs and elbows.

They double stitched and added patches
Around the knees and the exhaust,
Sewed zigzags where the head attaches,
But the brain - alas! – was lost.

They stuffed acorns where there had been brains
Which worked as well as the missing ones,
So when they did find his mental remains
They just tucked them between his buns.

APUT'S MAMMOTH

An Eskimo named Aput
Was amazed as anyone
To discover an elephant's foot –
A boy *mammoth,* thawing   out in the sun!

He scraped off snow and exposed
The whole beast, on a rocky outcrop.
To save it from getting decomposed
He fixed a lightning rod on top.

Wouldn't you know? A lightning storm
Awoke the mammoth, like Frankenstein.
How 'bout that? All friendly and warm!
Aput could see dollar signs.

But Universities, Foundations,
Even Research Corporations
Offered zilch, to his dismay.
They told him to go away!

"We have grants for mammoth study,
Good for 20 years or more!
We don't want answers, buddy!"
And they showed him out the door.

So **Big Money** is on the wrong track,
But you or I could give this a whirl.
They won't bring mammoths back
Until somebody finds a girl.

THE WORM OUROBOROS

Did humans invent the wheel?
Are there records to this effect?
There must be claims. It's a big deal.
But they would all be incorrect.

Snakes invented the wheel instead.
And they knew what they did. They said so.
Wait – I take that back. They never *said*.
I should have said they *meant* to.

Probably a prehistoric snake
Looked at herself, as a whole,
And thought, "I'll grab my tail and make
A big circle – and just roll!"

Every hoop snake down through the years
Has improvised this invention.
But when they try to brag to their peers
There is sudden apprehension.

See, snake teeth curve back to hold their prey.
Snakes did invent the wheel, no doubt.
But no hoop snake will ever say
Because they can't spit the tail out.

THE DEVIL SNAKE

While we're on the subject of snakes,
(Please refer to previous page)
One of them caused big headaches
In the First Biblical Age.

The snake offered Adam and Eve
An apple of the forbidden tree,
No doubt leading them to believe
A small sin – maybe *all* sins – are free.

After that flubber, sin was for sale.
But what if they'd haggled about that?
Like, "We'll eat it if you eat your tail".
Who could argue? That's tit-for-tat.

The devil wanted sin and heartache
So he'd be tempted to go that route.
He might have been the first hoop snake,
Stuck forever in 'Time-out'.

THE SOUTHERN BORDER

Half a dozen Mexican dragons
Decided to better their lives.
Their luck down there had been laggin'
So they headed north with their wives.

They walked with the other fake peasants
Across the actual border,
'Cause peasants are showered with presents
And the airspace is closed by Court Order.

Our Border Patrol served as greeters.
ICE handed out debit cards.
There were taxis without any meters,
Plus free lawyers. There were no guards.

When night fell, secret airliners
Boarded 'peasants' who had the most dough.
Everyone claimed they were minors.
But the dragons had to fly 'cargo'.

They landed right where they hoped to.
A sign said, 'Home of Joe's BBB'.
That had to mean 'Big Boy's Barbeque'.
They were in Washington, DC!

SUGAR AND SPICE

The problem with fairy tales,
Or even nursery rhymes,
Is translation of language details
From how they were used in Old Times.

Like the cute 'sugar and spice' ditty.
From when there were lots of mermaids.
Clearly, some translation committee
Made unscientific upgrades.

That was never about human girls,
Although there *are* sugar and spice ones.
It meant mermaids down by the pearls.
The girls with the cute, finny buns.

There's still sweet mermaids in the ocean
But their spices are a spicier kind.
So now a fair judge of their motion
Would notice more motion behind.

As for 'frogs, snails and puppy dog tails',
That sounds like boy turtles. Reptiles.
Are mermen born with shells and scales?
Maybe. Boy turtles have lovable smiles.

THE COVID ICON

What if you could *see* Covid Bugs?
Microscopic, floating free.
Contagious, dirty little thugs.
Wake up, pal. They're right on TV!

They're in newsrooms, hiding in plain sight!
Unseeing anchors broadcast
Emergency orders day and night
As the actual bugs float past.

We are told to mask downtown
As if that keeps things sterile.
That's misinformation. Calm down.
Back home is where you're in peril.

Just flip on your TV and wait.
Almost any channel you choose
Will soon have a Covid update
And you'll catch the bug from your news!

You'll find your TV screen
Is no more protection than a mask.
The dirty bugs slip through unseen.
Science can't explain, so don't ask.

The best way to flatten the curve
Is to shut off your TV, okay?
Ditch your mask. Have some spinal nerve.
Go out and live the old-fashioned way!

THE GREAT WALL OF CHINA

If the Emperors had built a wee wall
With legos from birthday presents,
China today would have all
Of *two* – not just one billion peasants.

The other billion went for dragon food
For guarding the Great Wall construction.
Until the Mongol Horde was subdued,
That was a bookkeeping deduction.

That price soured the Emperor's mood.
He'd rather pay cash by the hour.
The dragons loved their peasant food,
But it cost too much manpower.

He cut their rations by two thirds,
Unreasonably businesslike.
A huge pay cut, in other words.
So the dragons went on strike.

Sigh, labor demands through five dynasties
Over almost two thousand years
Made it tough even for the Chinese
To find enough volunteers.

But all clouds have a silver lining.
China's still a populous nation.
That excessive dragon dining
Saved them from *over*-population.

EMPTY SHELVES

It used to be common in Russia.
Hardly any bread on the shelves.
Some days not even *this-a-mucha.*
I think Big Shots ate it themselves.

Now there's bare shelves in Venezuela,
Another country that's poorly run.
It's just wrong when leaders live gala
And the people need food – and there's none.

That never happened in the U.S.
Except once when there was an issue
From a TV joke, no less,
That caused a run on toilet tissue.

Now – no baby formula! Who did *that?*
Why, our very own FDA.
They shut down a baby food plant whereat
They made formula every day!

It happens. There are so many rules.
But these bums had no backup plan
To cover the shortage, the fools!
That's like no tissue next to your can!

It's child abuse! Good sense unheeded!
Let's make 'em pay! How about this zinger?
Until they find the milk that's needed
They can wipe their fannies with their finger!

HYENAS

We must protect the great carnivores!
Or relocate them, in the long run.
Most countries would open their doors.
But not for hyenas - not one!

As a citizen in good standing
I volunteer the United States!
Listen up, DC! I'm *demanding!*
Open the immigration gates!

We have lots of nice gangland habitat
For hyena gangs to roam in.
Chicago is a nice city that
Hyenas could feel at home in.

For honest work they could
Sell laugh tracks to Hollywood.
Or crunch some bones in Washington.
That would benefit everyone!

Don't let this get stuck in committee.
Let's bring in hyenas. Let's push hard!
I volunteer my state, my city!
Just not my own backyard.

HAGS BY THE NOSE

Most woods will have scrub thorn trees.
Some dense, impenetrable tangle
Where humans, even on their knees,
Can't get in from any angle.

That's serious. It could be *hag brush*,
And infect the whole woodlot.
Is the momma bush a hag bush?
You must find out what you've got!

This all starts innocent enough
When a Night Hag idles barefoot.
In case you don't know this stuff,
Her feet and long nose can take root.

She'll look tree-ish now, the old bag.
You must tickle her – but not on the nose,
Or she'll sneeze if she *is* a Night Hag,
And break loose! Then anything goes.

Seven years bad luck if she sees you!
And she will. They wake up wide-awake.
Too late then to fix your boo-boo.
But what other course could you take?

You could sic your dog in, on a whim,
To mark her foot as his territory!
She'll curse even worse – but at *him,*
And you'll live to tell the story.

CREDIT CARDS

Dragons *do* eat us. Not funny!
But more than just roasts on a fire,
They see us as a way to make money
By financing our every desire!

So that's how loan sharking began.
At least in the United States.
It was dragons who worked out the plan
To loan money at illegal rates.

They upgraded that sleazy franchise
To a totally legal scheme.
A much richer enterprise:
Credit cards! Every shopper's dream.

By lobbying new usury laws
And raising card interest rates steep,
They made zillions, but for a good cause:
To build dragon treasure heaps!

So that's the gist of the story.
There's no need to be lawbreakers.
You can get rich and wave Old Glory
If you buy enough lawmakers.

ATTRAP, FATHER OF SPIDERS

Attrap was not meant to be here,
But became the First of Spiders
Conjured by the Magician Sehir
Through a mirror to the Dark Siders

Back then, immigration by magician
Or any other sneak-in or sniggle
Was still punished for lack of permission.
So spiders are all illegal!

But when the mirror welcomed Attrap
It stayed wide-open, like a door.
And being a clever chap,
He invited some friends. A lot more.

So our world wouldn't be overrun
By bums and unemployed rejects
A charm was taught to each one:
'The allurement of flying insects'.

That helped. Now they work for their food.
That's like jobs. They're respectable now.
But some are poisonous, dude!
So we stomp on 'em all anyhow.

WOOD NYMPHS

Ever go wood nymph viewing?
Of course you won't catch a glimpse.
The pastime is not worth pursuing.
But they're watching *us*, those nymphs!

The active spirit of their tree,
They appear as leaves or bark.
Unstudied, since they're hard to see.
But they've seen your hidden birthmark.

So you might think about *that*
When you 'go behind a tree'.
But it's the least of what they check out.
They also watch your TV!

Their network of tree roots was always
A homegrown telephone vine.
But it's vastly expanded these days
Since the roots touched your cable landline.

Now these nymphs listen in
To your phone conversations, dear.
How long until they begin
To beep out what they don't want to hear?

There should be a law! But there ain't.
It's tricky even calling the cops.
Best go wireless unless you're a saint.
Then only your government eavesdrops.

SHAMAL AND YAMIN

The Sorceress of the North Wind
Ice Queen of that frostbitten place
Grew tired of Shamal and Yamin
Throne Wolves who vied for her grace.

The two harbored mutual hate.
To settle it the Ice Queen said,
"The most valuable shall be First Mate.
I will see the other one dead".

Shamal, great conqueror, drove blizzard
After blizzard through the Hemisphere.
While sly Yamin, her Court Wizard
Whispered pieties in her ear.

We know she'd like a new Ice Age,
So Shamal is safe, that's clear.
But I'm sure Yamin can assuage
By whispering what she wants to hear.

Judging by our winter weather
Shamal's still alive, I would bet.
So my guess is, they're still together.
I don't think it's settled yet.

OLD RIPPER

The Elf Queen had gardens of flowers
As beautiful as they were big.
But even with all her powers
She couldn't save them from the wild pig.

Old Ripper brought about her downfall,
The son of Old Ironside.
Spears and arrows didn't hurt him at all
Because he had such a thick hide.

Years of wild animal wars
Convinced the Queen of the Elves
If they couldn't beat back wild boars
They would have to remove themselves.

She retired somewhere over the sea.
All the Elves embraced the same fate.
Which left fledgling humanity
With a free world to populate.

Old Ripper gave us that break,
So don't bellyache, Buttercup!
If garden pests keep you awake
Just smile and suck it up.

WHALES VS. GIANT SQUID

There is bloodshed under the sea
In the vasty deep, so it's hid:
A beneficial butchery
Where big whales eat giant squid.

That's great! Giant squid are eerie
And they live unnatural lives.
They weren't meant to be, is one theory,
Like ex-husbands and their ex-wives.

So how much squid do whales eat?
More than all other seafood!
Consuming that much is some feat.
To describe the discharge would be rude.

We *can* talk about their digestion.
Squid shells take powerful shredders.
How do whales avoid over-congestion?
You know it. They're Super Spreaders.

Oof da! How can the seas recover?
Oh, it's pretty safe. Don't panic.
Do analysis. You'll discover
The discharge is all organic.

THE SOUTH MOLE

'Twas a bad day for moles, still aboard,
When Antarctica broke free
From the big landmass northward
And headed for the Southern Sea.

No one else hung on as a martyr,
Just dumb moles, too slow to shift gears.
But the moles grew bigger and smarter
In the next 20 million years.

Then came polar explorers
Who planted the South Pole one night.
By morning, horror of horrors!
It was pulled underground out of sight.

It was moles, the rapscallions!
The researchers taught them language,
Which happened to be Italian,
And fed them Italian sausage.

The moles cleaned and kept logbooks
And learned to be like human moles.
Spying out the place like crooks
And smuggling were their goals.

First chance, they stowed away
On a cargo ship, very wittily,
Became 'Boat People' as they say,
And sneaked into Mother Italy.

After 20 million years or so
Giant moles are loose on earth!
And *we're* the only ones who know.
Holy cow! How much is that worth?

THE WHITE MAMMOTHS

Things have changed in the far north
From just 10,000 years ago.
It was bustling then, but thenceforth
Very quiet. Not much except snow.

No mammoths! They're working on hybrids
But they wouldn't quite be the right ones.
What a shame there's no mammoth grandkids.
But there are! A herd of all-white ones.

Where else but in Siberia?
They faithfully follow the Snow Elves.
They find grass, but there's no cafeteria
For either the Elves or themselves.

Probably the Great Spirit
Gave the herd seasonal color change
And a Divine Breeze to follow near it
And cover their tracks on the range.

If they need any more concealing
The Snow Elves won't fool around.
They can fade anything that's revealing -
Except piles of poo on the ground.

What about *that?* It's everywhere.
It invites interpretation.
Luckily, experts in armchairs
Are achieving clarification.

"Relics exposed by Global Warming".
That explanation will win it.
But Trappers who've seen the flies swarming
Say, 'It's fresh, and don't step in it!"

THE BERMUDA TRIANGLE

Some questions there is no answer to,
Some mysteries hard to untangle.
But let's pull something out of the blue
For the Bermuda Triangle.

To disappear huge ships or planes
On a perfectly nice afternoon
Would take tremendous force – and some brains,
Like the Boss of the Sea: Neptune!

As a cultured Roman divinity
He might wish for a planetarium,
And certainly show affinity
For a *reverse* aquarium!

He would collect air-breathers, plus
Our stuff, in a nice format,
So all his fish could look at us
In our natural habitat.

I say, let's just be delighted,
With a big exclamation mark!
That Captain Noah, the far-sighted,
Stayed away from there with his Ark.

THE MARTIANS

They looked a lot like humankind
And behaved somewhat the same
With a humanish cast of mind.
But then the Big Cool-down came.

Their old culture died. A cold wind blew.
Sand dunes covered every shred.
Their leaders didn't know what to do
So they followed gravity instead.

Down deep they lived on fossil bones.
When a million years had gone by
They looked just like Chinese clones:
Handsome, but regimented and shy.

Then – wouldn't you know? Astronauts!
And of course, they were Chinese ones.
They mingled more than they ought
And the Martians shot 'em with their own guns.

By that time the Martians knew enough,
Being so much like the Chinese.
Rocket science may be tough,
But they picked it up with ease.

So they launched with maximum force
Toward Earth, where they planned to arrive.
The ship was a Tesla, of course.
Hands-free and easy to drive.

They landed near Beijing.
{As Americans this should inspire us)
When Xi asked, "What did you bring?"
They gave him a Martian virus.

FOUNTAIN OF YOUTH

Dragon sweethearts, secretly engaged
But too young to marry, forsooth,
Went eloping when they were teenaged
And took vows at the Fountain of Youth.

Not an official marriage, like most.
A Vice-Squad might call it 'bootleg'.
Anyhow, they drank a big toast
And reverted right back to the egg.

They won't hatch with no Mom to make them.
It takes a jolt on the Richter Scale.
They won't get it if Mom can't shake them.
But luckily, they got hail.

The youngsters hatched and went their own ways
But you could write a romantic song,
How they might meet again someday,
At the Fountain! Just don't wait too long.

The County is looking at a permit
And may soon make a decision
To drain that tract lickety split
And build a new subdivision.

DRAGON FIREFIGHTERS

You might ask, "For all the dragon fire,
Do they have their own Fire Department?
Is it one taxpayers admire?
Is dragon tax money well-spent?"

We can only give you the facts:
Yes, no and no. It's expensive.
There's two bums with long-term contracts
And work rules no one can make sense of.

But there was no one else to hire!
It's a lot to ask of a fire-breather
To actually put out a fire
And these two don't like it either.

They'll respond to blazing garbage dumps.
Those are fun, and fun is the goal.
Then they just sit on their rumps
And declare it 'out of control'.

That's about all they do except training.
They torch firebreaks every day.
But whenever it isn't raining
They expect overtime pay.

If their Station burns, however,
(Like everyone else desires)
Their jobs would be lost forever,
So they're quick to put out *those* fires.

LAWYERS

Most lawyers are beasts or bogeymen.
At least half are, that's pretty clear.
Call 'em vultures if you'd rather, then.
But I'll call them bogeymen here.

They make up most of the ruling class
Because they're so well-tutored.
But to any working lad or lass
They're just tomcats that should be neutered.

A frontier newspaperman wrote:
"Employees and employers
Would all be better off (and I quote)
If we hanged half of the lawyers!"

That's drastic, though it does make one laugh.
I'd say, just put half on a boat
To anywhere – but which half?
Well, that newspaperman might have wrote:

"One lawyer has no opportunity
In a quarrel between friends,
But two lawyers in a community
Will bleed that case from both ends".

So they're all the same! Just hit or miss.
And it's time America acts!
Oh – wait a sec. I have to do this.
I need one to do some contracts.

THE GOP ELEPHANT

Ancestors of the elephant
The great Mammoth and Mastodon
Ruled the land wherever they went,
Whatever the Ice Age brought on.

Same with our African species
And Indian elephants too.
They are true-hearted beasts with strong knees
That pure elephant blood flows through.

GOP elephants of today
Bear a pygmy pedigree,
And a price which donors must pay,
But the trumpet and proboscis are free.

They've become a hybrid pachyderm
Crossed with a rhinoceros.
It's hoped this won't last long-term,
But with rhinos nothing's preposterous.

Some don't carry the pygmy gene
And some do – there's no telling, alas!
But they aren't all as big as they seem.
Some are bloated with rhino gas.

When GOP uses the pygmy brain
And looks like the boob that the joke's on,
They can blame that gene they contain
For the gas that the whole party chokes on.

DONKEYS

Donkeys aren't always donkeys,
Or 'jackasses' if you prefer.
A lot of them are honkies
And other ethnics that occur.

They've been successful, in the main,
Sly, stubborn and mean!
They get their way again and again,
Since back in the Pleistocene.

Even so, there remains some chagrin
That American Democrats
Made donkeys their emblem back then
When they could have chosen rats.

Hey, no offense! Who could resist
That lovable donkey grin?
Just know if you get donkey-kissed
It's an election year you're in.

The rest of the time, donkeys poop.
Oh, they're neat, with flags on their lapels,
But with hooves of course, they can't scoop,
So you can clean up their street apples.

SLURMS (SIAMESE-SNAKES)

A Chinese scientist who meant well,
But was a humanitarian fool,
Evolved a new support animal
As a marriage counselling tool.

He spliced a cleavage site between
Two benign snake embryos
And got Siamese snakes who had been
Joined with just one anal outgo.

That's where the plan went wrong.
Have you ever waited 'on deck'
While an occupant farts and sings songs,
And you'd like to wring their neck?

The Siamese snakes turned vicious,
Unsuited to do support stuff.
The police rated them too malicious,
Even though they made dandy handcuffs.

So the scientist took great care
To isolate the risk he'd brought on.
There must be a safe bio-lab, but where?
Luckily, there was one right in Wuhan.

THE MONKEY'S UNCLE

Lots of boys like the monkey exhibit
And daydream of life in the jungle.
Some swing on the bars to ad-lib it
And get noticed by the Monkey's Uncle.

He's an old hoo-doo trader
Who works a student-exchange scam:
Monkey nephews for Second Graders!
Hardly anyone sees through the sham.

The nephews buckle down to homework
While Tubby and Elmer (in this case)
Are exchanged like clockwork
And vanish without a trace.

They're off to the jungle of Nanamoo
Where it's all vacation and desserts.
They get pop and bananas too.
And they never tuck in their shirts.

Then they learned what it's all about.
They saw spellbound boys on display.
Uncle gleefully called, "Time Out!"
And they joined his gargoyles that day.

Back home the nephews are doing well
In school, but Mom don't trust those squirts.
That's a start, but to break her boys' spell,
She must find them and tuck in their shirts!

Don't bet against Mom.

EASTER ISLAND

The Spirit of Easter Isle, Uhane
Had been forever lonely
In a paradise lush and sunny
She was the one and only.

So she broke out the Stone Head Giants.
But they behaved like newborns.
The result of her dabble in science
Was infants with voices like bullhorns.

No sweat. She moved to Plan B.
She knew there were people on the seas
Because the winds offered up free
Polynesian music on the breeze.

She traced a Polynesian girl
In the Western sky they could see,
And the Stone Heads gave it a whirl.
They called real loud for *"MOMM--EEEE!"*

IT blasted like thunder bombs.
Enough to make eardrums weep.
But it drew their Polynesian Moms,
And the Stone Heads went right to sleep.

Now life on the Isle moves faster.
Tourism is big today.
But don't wake the Heads! That's disaster.
They would drive all the tourists away.

CORONA VIRUS BATS

The Covid bats are blameless!
But now they're forever cursed
Because politics is shameless
And the innocents get it first.

So bats harbor virus bugs?
So what? They mind their own business.
They don't give us kisses and hugs.
Leave them alone! Just don't mess!

Yeah, right. Humans leave *nothing* alone,
Though we preen like Sir Galahad.
The bat cave scientists were known
To have motives both good – and bad.

They plucked Covid samples, honey,
With their medical poke and jab,
Wrapped them in U.S. tax money,
And sent them to a Red Army Lab.

The story's not pretty, is it?
It smells like the bat cave floor.
They claimed that's where the trail quit
But now a whistleblower has more.

A linguist at that laboratory
Reports that *their* bats only shrug
At the Covid-Pandemic story.
Because it wasn't *their* bug.

THE PYRAMIDS

In 2700 B.C.
Egyptians were wiping their brow
Moving pyramid blocks ain't easy
And the bosses didn't even know how.

"Square blocks! Sharp edges! Straight lines!"
Pharoah ordered the architect.
It caused shipping delays of all kinds.
A typical government project.

Instead of dragging blocks on the ground
The workers had a suggestion:
"We could roll 'em if we made 'em round".
But that was out of the question.

So the job took 20 years
Instead of about 10.
And the budget blew out their arrears
But still, Pharoah was pleased. And then –

The Queen was *not* happy,
So no one was happy. Moreover,
She decided square blocks looked crappy,
And had to be plastered over.

She oversaw the final stages
When the polishing was done.
The snapshots are lost to the Ages.
But they say it gleamed white in the sun.

Looking back at the historic feat,
If they had taken the workers' advice,
The whole job coulda been complete
In half the time and looked just as nice.

GLACIERS

The wind blows where it wants to blow.
The ocean flows where it wants to flow.
The earth does its own rock and roll.
Even glaciers have a mind and a goal.

Whatever moves has a good reason
Reached with due consideration.
(Except government, which is just breezin',
That's true in any nation).

So what do glaciers think about?
It's not the last **Ice Age**, sweetheart.
It's the next one that's coming, no doubt.
Just look at any **Ice Age** chart.

They show it could happen fast
In just a few lifetimes or so.
And we've learned in times not long past
That we can't grow food in the snow.

We *can* grow food in Global Warming.
Modern agriculture has shown that.
So what if it gets habit forming?
It works for human habitat.

But if the **Big Green Plan** *is* passed
And all the nations conform,
Remember to invest in gas.
It might be needed to keep us warm.

THE BIG BOSSY COW PLAN (FOR WORLD PEACE)

It just seems, with the world so warlike,
We should study what farmers do.
They have tricks to make critters smell alike
That might work in Ukraine too.

To this cause farmers could donate
Bloated cow corpses for world peace!
PETA could pay the air freight,
The U.N. could receive them in Greece.

Since time is of the essence
With the carcasses almost popping
And some showing luminescence
There can be no thought of stopping.

The transfer will be air-to-air.
With guidance from a proctology nurse.
She can dock the planes' rear ends with care,
Because U.N. planes fly in reverse.

High above the Ukraine fighting
They simply light an attached flare
And drop cows with precise bomb-sighting
To detonate in mid-air.

Done right, everyone gets splattered.
They smell like bothers again.
Their differences will have been shattered.
But they might declare war on the U.N.

THE HAIR STYLIST

The dragon hairdresser, Miss Frizzy,
Made a fortune off bald dragon girls.
Growth tonic sales kept her busy,
Because all of them wanted curls.

It was the Year of the Coiffure!
And all the young dragon lasses
From the audacious to the demure,
Attended Frizzy's beauty classes.

The boys got something new to admire,
And the girls, hardly begrudging,
Put up with their flirty smoke and fire
Which did cause some scorching and smudging.

Sadly, it worked just temporarily.
Frizzy found it in the local dump,
Banned for false ads, because primarily,
Side-effects moved the hair to the rump.

Frizzy was hauled in for trial
In some Court of their Government,
But the judge upheld her denial
Because girls should read the fine print.

Yet, it all led to something better.
To cover a hairy derriere
Skirts became a new pacesetter
And launched the Age of Outerwear!

THE GREAT RED SPOT

Have you ever had a pimple
That itched, and you couldn't scratch it?
That's Jupiter's issue, plain and simple.
Only your own itch can match it.

His Big Red Pimple can't be popped.
But it could turn volcanic.
If it shoots up a mess to be mopped
Jupiter's moons would panic.

One is inhabited, round the clock.
The moon Io abounds with Io-ans.
Some consist of solid rock
But most are molten **MAGA**-ans.

They are all orbiting together
Just above that red blunderbuss.
For now they have beautiful weather,
But they're calling for possible puss.

For centuries they've watched the pimple.
Which might even be an abscess.
When it pops, the solution is simple.
MAGA-ans can burn up the mess.

DRAGONS & VIKING SHIPS

They were named the *Dire Agon*,
No doubt for their terrible fire.
Vikings just called them *dragon*,
Since the beasts were obviously dire.

It's odd that ancient Viking lore,
Save what *Beowulf* may reveal,
Says little of dragons. Why not more?
Probably because they were real.

Norse gods like Thor and Odin were great
For their epic battles and mayhem,
But everyday dragons aggravate.
They'd probably rather forget them.

Yet there are clues they cooperated.
Both sides specialized in pillage.
The dragon's share was calculated
Whenever Vikings sacked a village.

So Vikings put up with the cutthroats.
It's not something they chose.
But dragon heads on their longboats
Spread fear among their foes.

Vikings paid a price for fame and glory.
Their heroes got hurt – but won, at least!
We see this in the Beowulf story.
The heroes always killed the beast.

But dragons were not considered beasts.
They were business partners. Allies.
They were invited to Viking feasts.
Norwegians are very wise.

GREMLINS

Fairy folk, as Children of the Light,
Had no shadows from creation.
They found them here, and also Night,
Because of earth's rotation.

So fairy shadows were an add-on,
Just related, like night and day.
No matter now, that's all bygone.
Because their shadows broke away.

The shadows awoke, tuned corporeal.
We call them gremlins now.
Little Rotters who lie, cheat and steal,
And get in your hardware somehow.

They still attract dark shadow
As mechanics are well aware.
They use trouble lights to throw
The troublemakers out of there.

You would call them viruses or bugs
In your electronic devices.
But it's gremlins acting like they're on drugs.
That's outrageous at today's prices!

In olden days when we sat down bare
To use our outdoor potties,
We suspected they hide below and stare,
So we wiped at them with Scotties.

Which brings up an interesting point,
A bathroom tip to make you frown:
Gremlins might be using the joint,
So check for shadows before you sit down.

HEAD HUNTERS

It's taboo today, as a rule,
But once there were civilizations
Where head-hunting and shrinking were cool,
Quite respectable occupations.

For good taste we'll simply delete
The hunter/gatherer part.
We'll just leave that incomplete
And skip to the head-shrinking art.

That's a witch doctor specialty.
Done right, the head keeps ticking.
A smart buddy, potentially,
And no fighting or kicking!

Pricey, but with low-maintenance charm.
They're noise polluters, but light eaters.
They make great burglar alarms
And even act as greeters.

The Big Chief who runs the town forum
Used them whenever he feared
He was gonna be short of a quorum
As his own people disappeared.

All too often, their tenure was brief.
Sometimes the heads did pretty good.
But they liked to vote against the Chief
Just because they could.

THE LOST DUTCHMAN'S MINE

Francisco Coronado
Searched for seven cities of gold,
The riches of El Dorado,
In New Mexico but came up cold.

Coronado thought it odd
That Native guides couldn't find the way.
But the gold belonged to their god,
So they always led him astray.

Over time the fabulous riches
Merged with tales of a Lost Dutchman's mine.
Lots of prospectors lost their britches
Seeking the hidden entrance sign.

But it's lost. The Dutchman dug too deep,
Unearthed the owner of the treasure:
A dragon, but thankfully asleep,
With gold and silver beyond measure.

He grabbed up all he could carry
And vamoosed from the dragon's hold.
But that night the beast would bury
The entrance, sevenfold.

There are still Native guides, and it's funny,
If you mention *Dutchman* they act shy.
Oh, they'll gladly take your money.
Just don't get your hopes up too high.

MAROONED ON A DESERT ISLE

What's the worst fate for a sailor?
Sure, marooned on a desert Isle.
It's like being your own jailer.
It gets worse. Stick around a while.

Meet Sam, the sole survivor
Of a deep diver boat explosion,
Because he was the deep diver.
Now he frets about beach erosion.

The Isle has a palm tree and fresh
      water
In a tidy, spring-fed pool,
Plus himself, a simple squatter.
The rest is hot sand. Not cool!

By day he climbed the tree for shade
And stayed like a bashful fool
All night as laughing mermaids
Washed their hair in the pretty pool.

They saw him and laughed at that
      too,
But each night they left him sushi,
Which he ate, as his hunger grew,
Until he must unload his tushy.

He did his business behind the tree
And covered it like a kitty.
But it didn't fool anybody.
Poor Sam received no pity.

The mermaids tattled to Neptune,
The Sea God, who said, "(bleep)"
And a wave washed over the sea dune
Sending Sam to the vasty deep.

So that's why mermaid beauties
Are called *mythic* and remain aloof:
They've been seen with their fishtail
      booties
But no one has lived to show proof.

GALAXIES

Have you ever had a pinwheel?
An actual sparkler one?
Then you've got a pretty good feel
How a galaxy gets spun.

I think I can safely say
The Great Spirit gives them a spin.
And possibly even today
There are worlds like ours therein.

But like pinwheels when they're depleted
And disappear into a trash bin
The galaxies are being deleted.
Black Holes are sucking them in!

We must change the way we behave
To make up for what Black Holes inhale!
There's a lot of stuff we could save
Just on our earthly scale!

Like this: Dumpsters will not be allowed!
We'll livestream our trash from afar
And upload it all to the Cloud!
Oh, wait. Is that where Black Holes are?

PENGUINS

Great Spirit liked them black-breasted
And they were meant for up north.
But the penguins protested
About polar bears, and so forth.

So He moved them to the South Pole
An uninhabited land
(Not counting the Great South Mole)
And reversed their polarity band.

That reversed their colors too.
They now would be white-bellied critters.
But they were free to do what they do
Until men fit them with transmitters.

I wouldn't care to be studied
Or tracked electronically.
My whims have a right to be muddied.
Same with penguins, ironically.

We're just like penguins anymore.
They've got us on live GPS.
They know what we're shopping for.
Even watch us from space, I guess.

But while penguins might someday have peace
If those studies are ever completed,
Our own freedoms will cease.
Some of us might just be deleted.

GHOST WARRIORS

We know who they are, or were:
The blood-thirstiest tribes of their day!
Aggressors like those still occur
In some countries now, by the way.

The ones in the Ghost Realm can see you
But they're watching our Upper Classes,
Jealous how now it's so easy to
Pacify the masses.

The old Aztecs? The Mongol Horde?
Their methods are way out of touch.
I heard they were put to the sword.
So they're history, pretty much.

Today there's no need for trophy heads,
Or any blood at all, what the heck?
That was fun, but today the Feds
Just use Media and Big Tech.

Times have changed from the bad old days.
New rulers have civilized ways.
What Ghost Warriors got with bloody skulls
Big Tech gets by making us numbskulls.

THE ROYAL MENU

It started with 'Meatless Mondays'
At the pretty Dragon Queen's request.
Soon they were serving baled hay
And every meal was a veggie fest.

Love does that – even to a Dragon King,
But the diet began to tell.
His gut became a huge, bloated thing.
Dragons don't digest grass very well.

For moments like this great chefs are born!
His bean soup, when things looked most grim,
Uncorked the robust Royal Horn,
Just as rebels arrived to dethrone him.

The conspirators were overcome.
Masked guards foiled the coup.
And the Queen went home to her Mum
While the castle aired out. So would you.

So there's a nugget of wisdom:
Allowing extra points for the smell,
It's just hard to beat the system.
They can always drop a bombshell.

THE CAVE MAN WAR

The Neanderthal or Cro-Magnan
Could not write out language as such.
But their cave art certainly can.
It's like speaking. That's a nice touch.

Thus we know what they liked and admired.
Beasts still leap, as if time stands still.
And their warriors, who never get tired
Slay foes! So we know who they killed.

But we're not the first to uncover
That evidence of cave man war.
It's a cave many would discover.
So who else might have been here before?

Maybe a gaggle of dragon toddlers
Being home-schooled by a dragon mum?
Imagine that bunch of dawdlers
All asking, "Why? How come?"

"They look different, so that's why they fight",
Explained teacher, shaking her head.
"Silly humans judge others by sight,
And it leads to a lot of bloodshed".

"But you'll learn that they're all nutritious.
It has nothing to do with their face.
All humans are simply delicious,
Regardless of color or race!"

CATS – OR DOGS?

As Great Spirit populated earth
And considered what else to send
He added cats, for what that was worth,
Thinking they could be Man's Best Friend.

That had to be all for now.
He must think of the Universe.
Great Works must be done somehow!
So He left, for better or worse.

To the Great Spirit, time passes slow.
But the earth was on Daylight Savings.
Things change quickly. Once cats were let go,
The big ones got raw human cravings.

Cuddly ones mooched what they could.
You could say Man was *their* best friend.
But they didn't fight for the common good.
Their food dish was all they'd defend.

Wolf dogs, who also got food,
Were more value to the young human race.
If saber-tooths snatched a cave dude
The dogs fought them face to face.

Sorry, cats think first of their gut.
They're not the best friend we could wish.
When there's trouble, all we see is their butt.
But they will come back to their dish.

MAMMOTH TRUNKS

Like so many old extinctions
The mammoths remain a riddle.
Well, they must have had mortal afflictions.
Let's solve this while experts twiddle.

We know they survived Ice Ages
Warm in their bulky masses
Swinging tusks of very broad gauges
To sweep the snow off the grasses.

But if snow was too deep for the brutes
Could they get food just with their trunks?
No. Compared to modern elephant snoots
It lacked one muscle, so their trunk flunks.

It had thousands, according to lore,
But they couldn't save one mammoth band.
Modern elephants have *one muscle more,*
That can pluck a peanut off your hand!

That was the mammoth's bad luck.
Starved of food, with empty guts,
Their big trunks were unable to pluck
The plentiful arctic hare peanuts.

AYERS ROCK

Ayers Rock, now known as Uhuru
Sits in the middle of nowhere
In the Australian Outback, true to
Aboriginal spirits who played there.

We accept that. Young dragons do too.
But it never stopped their rock concert.
Once a year, in a storm, right on cue
They blast music until their ears hurt.

Young dragons have rocked there forever.
Perhaps thousands of years ago,
The first Aborigines ever
Heard the first-ever beat of bongo.

So it goes way back, and the Rock
Is inverse to an amphitheater.
But it still might compare to Woodstock
With expanded decibel meter.

Young dragons aren't into pot,
So the crowd is different from Woodstock's.
But they do have beer that they got
From some guy back in the boondocks.

BRITISH CRIMINALS IN AUSTRALIA

Merry Old England had no pity
For even tuppence thieves.
Debtor's Prison in London City
Was stuffed with them to the eaves.

But after 1782
U.S. wouldn't take the overflow.
What could Merry Old England do?
Where could their poor wretches go?

Well, leave it to Merry Old King George
He still had Australia, so with ease
He ordered the prison to disgorge
The crooks even *farther* overseas.

That worked for everyone pretty well,
Except the Bushmen, of course.
But Merry Old England made the hard sell,
As usual, by force.

Let's wish both convicts and Bushmen well.
At least time has brought better things.
Australia is huge and they all can dwell
Without any Merry Old Kings.

I think the Merry Old USA
(Where shoplifters get off free
In some cities, by the way)
Should drink Merry Old English tea.

Let's deport our Merry Old Thieves!
Just ship them to overseas sites.
Let's cheer when a planeload leaves!
We'll call ''em *Merry Old Gangsta* flights.

THE GREAT FENCE OF AUSTRALIA

Not as famous as China's Great Wall
Because it's hidden Down Under,
But the Great Fence was meant to fix all
Their invasive species blunders.

Rabbits first. Us humans brought those.
Well, Merry Old King George did that.
Rabbits dug under as everyone knows.
They were smarter than us, and that's flat.

So? Anyone can blow it once!
That's sort of what humans are about.
But don't call an Aussie a dunce
Or you'll get your teeth knocked out.

They re-designed the Great Fence
To keep invasive dingo dogs at bay,
And to prove there *is* common sense
In Australia today.

(Not counting the last 2 years
When protesters sang from hymnals
To drown out the government's cheers
As they locked up Covid 'criminals'.)

But dingoes have run free forever.
Even the Bushmen agree.
So why call them invasive, or whatever?
Who can say they shouldn't run free?

Maybe Bushmen were seagoing traders
Who discovered that island/nation.
Should we still call them invaders?
Nope. There's a statute of limitation.

My grandparents sailed too, back when.
As migrants they were roundly despised.
But they were viewed as born again
When they got naturalized.

POLAR BEARS

Great Spirit created a Lion King.
But he was a night-loving one.
So Bears, who were the very next thing,
Ruled the earth under the sun.

There were black bears aplenty
And brown bears would play a huge role
But the Arctic was still bear-free.
He needed some at the North Pole!

He made extra-big brown ones
For those lands of ice and snow,
But right away they gobbled tons
Of penguins – until He said, "NO!"

Clearly, penguins couldn't stay there
Where they were sitting ducks.
As we know now, He sent them elsewhere
The bears said something like, "Oh, shucks".

"You will eat the plentiful seals",
He consoled them. "That's your birthright".
But they headed south for easier meals
So He painted all of them white.

That's how Great Spirit won the day.
White bears stayed where they fit in better.
And He cautioned them, by the way,
Not to use those words with 4 letters.

UNICORNS OF THE SEA

Are we related to mermaid girls?
Doubtful, though their lower section
Can do human-like wiggles and whirls.
But there is a common connection.

Like humans who, historically,
Were saved from dragons by unicorns,
Mermaids also, categorically,
Owe their lives to unicorn horns.

You can pretend the world is well-behaved
If that soothes your emotions,
But it gets bloody, and mermaids *were* saved
By the unicorns of the oceans.

Narwhals with their stabbing horn
Made hungry dragons wary.
They hate dragons from the day they're born.
Mermaids are the beneficiary.

Lucky for those girls! They would be missed
By guys lucky enough to see them,
And it leaves a chance to *prove* they exist!
(Or *exist,* if you happen to be one.)

THE SUPREME OCTOPUS

I once had a pet octopus
Who behaved pretty well I would say.
He did have 9 arms, which was surplus,
But the odd one could reach either way.

One day he started raving,
Spitting food and talking smack.
The neighbors saw him misbehaving
So I dressed him all in black.

I have a small house – what could I do?
He needed space; don't you agree?
So I pawned him off to the zoo
In Washington, D.C.

But he needed even *more* space
As his arms kept growing,
So he took over a much bigger place
Without anyone knowing.

From there he could reach sea to sea!
The whole country was his oyster.
But he proceeded to spit food and pee
All over his Supreme Court cloister.

So now there's no clean trail
To justice. It's a bog.
The Supreme Octopus is the tail
That wags the whole government dog.

Can we tame him? It might soon be tried.
Some want to give the big brat
Four more arms, all on one side.
Hmm. We might think twice about that.

But since he acts like a god,
And a god-like octopus is a sham,
He needs a warning sign on his bod.
Like a witches pentagram.

ISLE OF THE AMAZONS

There was always an Amazon Isle
In the heyday of piracy
Where rich girls lived a rough lifestyle
Until Daddy paid the ransom money.

An old dragon mum, Ms. Buns,
Ran it with an iron fist.
All pirates, even human ones,
Were on her waiting list.

It was a lot like Ranger School,
Overrun by spiders and gnats.
They ran laps through an open cesspool.
A great place to cure spoiled brats.

But a funny thing happened with time.
Rich parents started *sending* their kids.
Paying right up front, every dime.
Now Ms. Buns is taking bids.

The good old pirates are gone. Au Revoir!
Good old piracy seems to be dead.
But we'll know she's gone too far.
If the island goes co-ed.

MOTHER NATURE

Great Spirit liked the new earth, pretty much
Except for one important detail.
It lacked a woman's touch.
But then – the heart turned out to be female!

Thus Mother Nature made her debut.
She would be earth's surrogate Mom.
But He awoke four stepchildren too,
And that was the end of the calm.

The step kids were the Four Winds.
They would do weather, with Mom's advice.
The East and West Winds were wunderkinds.
But the North and South weren't as nice.

That didn't please their stepmom at all.
But the Great Spirit meant it so.
The winds must fight, or no rain will fall.
Without that, nothing will grow.

So our assurance of stormy weather
Depends on contrary attitudes
Of winds that can't live together
But won't stay at their own latitudes.

Can *our* Moms find wisdom here, or morals?
Some help for rebel daughters or sons?
Well, Ms. Nature is stuck with her quarrels,
But we can send our kids to Ms. Buns.

THE BUGABOO

Dark closets, dim attics, the shadow.
Unlit places raise our suspicions.
A thought pops up: "You never know…"
We can't help our premonitions.

But why? It just makes no sense.
This is earth! Are not humans supreme?
Have we no means of self-defense?
Then why this recurring daydream?

You know it's just a bugaboo,
A phony hallucination,
A figment. But it seems so true!
Is it only imagination?

Or is it a memory of shadow
Where Dire Wolf and Sabretooth
Laid in wait for us long ago?
More likely, that's the truth.

Or, following that reasoning,
It's probably their ghosts,
Since there are no living offspring.
Well! Let's show them we're not milquetoasts!

We are the modern King of Beasts!
Fear not! We're rough and tumble!
See me? I'm not scared in the least!
The torch is just so I don't stumble.

CUBICLES

Ever notice how soft we've become?
We drive cars with A/C's to work.
With heated seats for our bum.
Maybe company-owned, as a perk.

We still need *some* blue-collar slobs,
But cubicles are taking over.
Compared to manual jobs
Office work is a bed of clover.

It's soft. That makes slobs like me grin.
We once had a country whereof
Pioneers had no pot to pee in,
Or windows to throw it out of.

Fortunate guys built log houses
With bare hands or borrowed tools
For their 12 kids and lovely spouses
And the kids walked miles to the schools.

And some homes were just blocks of sod,
Or rough lean-tos. Now that's bumming!
But even big families, thank God,
Had sufficient outdoor plumbing.

Reducing this to analogy,
That cubicle where you may have sat?
Well, a lot of older families
Had outhouses bigger than that.

THE AURORA

The Northern Lights burst in aura.
The Northern Lights look like a curtain.
We can explain the great Aurora,
But what's behind it is less certain.

That won't change. It isn't meant to.
The Great Curtain will stay drawn.
Fairy folk do not intend to
Let us snoop where they have gone.

Most of them have now forsaken
The crowded earth. They're gone with their light.
Not our fault, but fairies have taken
To the Night Sky, out of reach, out of sight.

That much is known from Witchlore.
It greatly pleased the witches.
Until pixies came back for an encore.
It's hard to shake those little snitches!

They're mischief, the pixie girls are.
For witches, that's nothing new.
And if you stick *your* nose in too far,
They'll be happy to tweak that too!

ELECTRIC EELS

We must move to electric cars!
Because – Bless 'em! – they save the planet.
So I'm saving up to buy ours.
But I'll need to burn gas til they ban it.

That's fine. It gives one time to think.
Are there flaws? The Greenies should list 'em.
Do EV's have any missing link?
Yep, a renewable recharge system.

So without giving too much away,
And avoiding speech diarrhea,
I shall patent electric eels one day!
How's that for an idea?

You'll place a small tank of water
Near your battery. That's all you do.
Add one eel (say you legally caught her).
Jumper cables connect the two.

Of course, an eel eats and craps,
So flush if there's any emission.
You can feed them your table scraps
That will keep them in fine condition.

I'll get rich like the oligarchs
When this takes over the nation!
And you'll all smile, happy as larks
As you cruise past the charging station!

BATTERIES

Had a bad thought a moment ago.
What if people don't like my eels?
Will EV's go the way of the dodo?
Would that doom electric wheels?

No! Where there's a will, there's a way!
Gas prices are already high,
But goose 'em higher, OK?
Say, $10 in the sweet by-and-by.

We'll build tax-paid charging stations
That gas guzzler guys can pay for
At inconvenient locations
Which no one will ask your OK for.

If EV prices cause a bank run
Don't worry! Just mortgage your house, and,
You'll be able to buy a cheap one
For only fifty thousand!

Oh, wait. Batteries. China has those.
They mine the rare earth to make 'em.
Almost no one else has 'em, goodness knows.
So we're just beholden to take 'em.

But that's the same gang, for certain,
Who laughed at us and had the gall,
To smart off when we were hurtin':
"We might withhold your Tylenol!"

We have rare earth in California
If they would just let our miners dig.
We can't get everything from China,
Or they'll roast us like a fat pig.

THE HANGING GARDENS OF BABYLON

Nebuchadnezzar was a tyrant.
His Daddy was that way too.
He was raised as a tyrant-aspirant.
So what else was he going to do?

When he, himself, became King
He learned to worry about his beans.
Assassination was the in-thing
And poison was the usual means.

All were at risk, the tyrants of the day
For toxins in their milk and honey.
But Neba was better off than they,
Because he had way more money!

He built expensive hanging gardens,
And picked his own veggies and fruit.
Plus, in lieu of issuing pardons,
He hanged his old chefs to boot.

He was never poisoned like he feared.
He ruled for 43 cruel years.
But his cause of death, it appeared,
Was a blunt force between the ears.

DRAGON REST HOMES

Where do all the old dragons go
When they get long in the tooth?
Some quiet rest home for the afterglow?
Would you believe that's the truth?

They know when their fire starts to die out
They have less than a century.
They can choose a rest home for checkout
Or the dragon penitentiary.

Most ladies opt for the rest home
And the geezers follow the chicks.
But the guys are locked in a padded room
To bitch about politics.

Ha-ha! Will you believe anything?
Male dragons are very strong-willed.
They don't do the rest home thing.
They just live until they're killed.

Girls too! Ignoring fashion details,
They're just as tough as the males.
They pillage too, and plunder
And blast out gas like thunder,
But they always have beautiful nails.

EXTRA-TERRESTRIAL LIFE

The asteroid came into view.
The landing site was almost bare.
Great! The lander could pick through
A few flat rocks here and there.

So Mission Control sent it down
To drill samples of this and that.
The surface was green, the rocks
    were brown.
Everything was tested and poked at.

The flat rock samples were found
To the shock of space scientists –
To be an organic compound!
That put their underwear in a twist.

The compounds were life's building
    blocks,
Which meant they might be alive!
If an old 5th planet broke into rocks
Were these survivors of that planet 5?

Anyhow, this was all broadcast live
And millions of people just froze
As the spacecraft did a power dive
And the cameras zoomed in close.

NASA scientists were thrilled!
This would lead to more missions.
Their ambitions would be fulfilled
With promotions and new positions!

The camera panned the landing site
While they debated the aliens.
There was even some level of fright.
What if they were mammalians?

In Wisconsin that conversation
Faced a more critical eye.
Farmer Ole muttered, "Tarnation!
That lander's gonna step in a pie".

Farmer Ole milked Brown Swiss
And he wasn't fooled by manure.
"Lena!" he said. "Come see this!
They're showing an old cow
    pasture".

snogg and the hoo

Only natural forces stop rainstorms.
New atmospheric conditions.
Rain might stop if the air cools or warms
Or moves on to new positions.

Blizzards are more superficial
About following natural laws.
They act natural in the initial,
But end from an unnatural cause.

That's due to two personalities.
Have you heard of Snogg and the Hoo?
They always had different moralities
That determined which way the wind blew.

Snogg brings the North Wind, he makes the snow.
Each flake is unique because –
That's the rule! When inspiration runs low,
Naturally, he must pause.

He starts again from the beginning
So the next snowflake is a repeat.
The Hoo sees this and starts grinning.
The snow ends, because Snogg cannot cheat.

The Hoo was sent by the South Wind
To stop him. She likes it warm.
So the first and last flakes are twinned,
The only two alike in the storm.

ELEPHANT BIRDS

They say eggs are going up again.
Some bird flu I guess, or a drought.
The Market will tell us how much and when.
Just follow your budget printout.

It's that easy in the Computer Age,
But Maoris had no calculators.
They didn't even have minimum wage.
But they still wanted eggs with their taters.

The Maoris couldn't know, as they ate
Scrambled eggs in a forest clearing,
With no I-Phones to extrapolate
That Giant Moas were disappearing.

So let's excuse the old stories
And tribes with no I-Phones or PC's.
We mustn't blame the old Maoris
For wiping out delicious species.

Shucks, what's done is done. Let's condone
Everyone, and their Dad and Mum.
'Cause they didn't invent the cell phone
Til everyone had cars to text from.

PIRANHA FISH

Right now if I had one wish,
Anything I could wish from above,
I need a hungry piranha fish
For this rat they want a skeleton of.

At least we all got the assignment,
So I'm not suffering alone.
But this rat is out of alignment.
My dog crunched his backbone.

Why didn't he just eat it?
That's the classic way to cheat.
It's a great excuse. You can't beat it.
I would've got 'Incomplete'!

I would never take Biology,
But it's a required class.
Ugh, now it's leaking! Is this Urology?
It gets worse. The carcass has gas.

Phew! Bad gas. I would've started
Much sooner, had I known!
Must remember to write 'Farted'.
The report should be full-blown.

Oh Homework Saints, send piranha
If it's within your power!
My rat needs skinning, and I don't wanna!
And the skeleton's due next hour.

DRAGON DOLLS

Where are the darling dragon dolls
That should be in our stores
So girls could blast make-believe fireballs
And pretend bloody dragon wars?

They say there's a lack of demand.
They say a typical girl adores
2-legged human dolls with hands.
Not dolls that walk on all fours.

Well, dragon girls like those too.
However, they prefer them alive.
And more than just one or two,
Because some of them don't survive.

So if you're grabbed by a dragon mum
On your way to the Mall
And her brat is a girl, you'll become
Her cuddly human doll.

A lot depends on the daughter.
If she turns out to be strict
With dolls her Mum has brought her,
Follow orders, or she'll get ticked!

And if you don't do things quite right?
You'll get spanked, to be precise.
Or she'll remember her appetite.
So behave. Above all, play nice!

For rich 'dolls' there's a chance of ransom.
There's nuthin' wrong with hopin'.
Til then, just let her be 'Mum'.
Don't argue when she says, "Open!"

THE FISH OF ETERNITY

One pair of giant fishes
In the Seas of the First Age,
Ate all the others against the wishes
Of the Great Spirit, who was outraged.

When fat Riba and his mate Kala
Retired to a deep hole
Near what is now Venezuela,
He made an Almighty Fishing Pole.

He arranged the stars to make *Angill*,
An Almighty Fisherman
To catch them out for the grill.
A sure and simple plan.

Angill cast a lure no fish should ignore.
Riba snubbed it. Kala was picky.
He tried every lure in the Evermore
With no luck. Fishing is tricky.

He finally cast a squiggly worm
And hooked the old girl with live bait.
Fish just can't resist things that squirm.
But this also sealed Angill's fate.

When he reeled her up to the sky
Her mate leaped up and swallowed him, see?
The lovers became stars, by and by:
The *Fish of Eternity.*

SKUNK CABBAGE

Way back in the First Age of earth,
When skunks were called *the Skagon,*
When they practiced old-fashioned childbirth,
They smelled sweet! But those days are gone.

When the Winter of the North Wind
Overwhelmed the hemisphere
The starving Skagon were destined
To eat the *Kagnabag.* Oh, dear.

The plant is horribly foul-smelling.
It's cabbage-like, but hollow.
It didn't take much fortune telling
To know that bad luck would follow.

The Skagon were hauled before the throne
Of the Sorceress of the North.
She bewitched them with a joke all her own.
Then she laughed and sent them forth.

At last she was defeated
And Spring was celebrated that year.
But the Skagon had been cheated.
Their sweet babies did not appear.

They turned up in the Kagnabag whorls.
Blame the Sorceress, we think.
Smelly boys and, alas, smelly girls!
That's how they got skunk cabbage stink.

PRAIRIE DOG TOWNS

When cities in America
Come up short on law and order,
Prairie dog towns might merit a
Closer look (Those north of the border).

Is there angst in our cities today?
Guys who just act barbarian?
Carnivores are like that, but they say –
Prairie dogs are vegetarian!

No dog is stronger than the next dog.
The grass diet brings hormones down
About on par with a lap dog.
There's no outlaws in prairie dog town!

They have a whistle warning system
And if predators approach
They never, ever resist 'em.
Prairie dogs just let 'em poach.

They are also a gun-free zone.
No one breaks the rule, not one trifle.
But from long range they are blown
Away by sporting rifles.

Transportation is safely on foot.
But the overcrowded paths do rankle.
Some rude dogs just don't give a hoot.
And the potholes! You could break an ankle.

Hmm. Maybe the great prairie dog
Ain't so great after all. Mama mia!
Well, so much for that analog.
We still need a better idea.

THE SPEED OF DARKNESS

If you divided the universe
Between light and dark, on a graph,
Estimating how light will disperse,
What would you get? Half and half?

So that's some idea of quantity.
But which has the greater speed?
That puts experts in a quandary.
"Shade is passive", they will plead.

They're wrong. I'll do a demonstration.
I'm not even a trained scientist.
But because I have less education,
I see some things that they've missed.

Without getting into Black Holes
I can just show you in clips
That the speed of darkness rocks and rolls.
There is proof in every eclipse.

You can measure the speed of dark
Overtaking the light of the sun!
This should settle that question mark.
Any more questions, anyone?

For more proof, check with your government.
They have long known light is losing out.
Our Daylight-Saving Time is meant
To stall off the coming blackout.

THE COMMON COLD

Turns out that the Covid hype
Was totally overblown.
For dragons, with their body type,
It's worse to catch a common cold.

The cold comes on superficially
And turns into deadly disease.
The worst symptom initially
Is expressed as a violent sneeze.

Such a blast can set forests ablaze
So stand back from the dragon's snout.
But this first, most virulent phase,
Will likely blow his own fire out.

That's bad. A cold dragon will die
Without some regeneration.
They need a hot dragon to try
Mouth to mouth resuscitation.

Please! A fiery oral snort!
But it's such an embarrassing sight.
So – no volunteers? As a last resort
There is medical dynamite.

DRAGON MAIL

Today, most marauding firedrakes
Have moved north to new stomping grounds.
Our kids may never hear the *"BOOM!"* it makes
When dragon fire breaks the speed of sound.

This did cause consternation
Up north, at Santa's Workshop,
Which has a large population,
And all their work came to a stop.

The worst dragon, Old Blacktooth Jack,
Was about to chow down an elf,
But Jack set him carefully back
At a stern look from Santa himself.

A deal was struck. Dragons stayed there.
They fired up stoves and hauled mail.
Gifts too, during the Covid scare,
So that Santa would never fail.

First Princess feeds them fish each day -
No job for wimps. The fish are stinky,
And the dragons snap at her in play.
The Princess is down to one pinky.

Santa stays old-fashioned. That's neat.
He has no Twitter handle. That's true.
If he did, he would probably tweet:
"Times change, but we're still here for you!"

THE FIRST DATE

You remember, I know you do,
When you met your in-laws-to-be.
Young dragons also tiptoe through
Each other's Family Tree.

Dragon mums are very suspicious.
The boyfriend must somehow charm her!
And to show Pop he's ambitious
Bring a gift: A live knight-in-armor!

Oh – not a Knight of the Round Table!
But some young knight-in-training.
Just so he has the label.
He's being paid. The guy is feigning.

Feigning? Yes, faking. Pop knows it.
It's a charade to make peace.
Boyfriend looks good, Pop don't expose it.
But it's secretly catch-and-release.

Mum wants to see the bachelor cave.
This marriage thing strikes her as risky.
The girls leave, so will the boys behave?
No. Pop gets out the whiskey.

If the lad holds his booze, he'll be fine.
It's time to drink and answer questions.
And it's best if he has a good shine
When the ladies return with 'suggestions'.

army ants

If you're in your hut in the Amazon
When the army ants march to your door,
And you shut it because you aren't a moron,
And squish those that come through the floor –

You're normal! I'm glad to meet you!
You defend your way of life.
And if jaguars try to break through
I'll bet you carry a knife!

More likely, all the villagers
See the ants coming from their porches.
And you're used to fighting off pillagers,
So you're ready with fire and torches!

Our U.S. protects nothing anymore.
We seem to be overrun by mobs.
No one protects our front door,
Not to mention our back door or jobs.

A village needs one or two rules.
You don't need to have a lot.
But don't open your doors like fools
To just anyone who wants what you've got.

WITCHES

The devil always had some grip.
Since Adam and Eve, probably.
So witchcraft and devil worship
Were just signs of his malignancy.

Witches were a little worse
Than pagan religions in those days.
They spread the devil's curse
In many different ways.

Human sacrifice was their style.
(Please allow me to call them 'Bitches'.)
It led to the Salem witch trial
And open season on witches.

That's when things really got nasty.
Neighbors ratted out neighbors
To be burned at the stake. It was ghastly.
And some for just innocent labors.

The devil probably said, "Oops".
So he lost a few witches. Who cares?
There are always more nincompoops
Willing to take up his affairs.

But witches are underachievers.
I've read where, no matter how clever,
They are something that True Believers
Won't have to put up with forever.

THE TERRA COTTA ARMY

What is it with despotic monarchs?
They build monuments for us to see.
The pyramids were the benchmark,
But now comes Emperor Shi.

First Emperor of all the Chinese!
He set a record for going in style:
An underground *city* if you please,
That covers 20 square miles.

He has an army around him:
7000 fearsome clay warriors!
Lifesize, fully armed and grim.
(Thanks to underpaid clay quarriers.)

Shi was a megalomaniac
But the prospect of death did scare him.
Poor guy needed comfort, demanded in fact
To be buried along with his harem.

Like Hitler, he practiced historic theft -
Slew scholars, burned books & libraries.
We know this because no one was left
To whitewash his obituaries.

I guess the army was for protection.
He had old foes, so he's gotta.
Just one thought, upon reflection:
Can they fight? The answer is *nada.*

TAX FREEDOM DAY

Tax Day is April 15, as a rule –
But this year it's the 18th, they say.
How could they be so darn cruel?
That's supposed to be Tax *Freedom* Day!

The idea is a quick, sure fix
With much-needed strong medicine
For irresponsible politics
And the financial mess we're in.

If your whole paycheck went in the latrine,
Excuse me! I meant *Treasury,* dear.
It would take until April 18
To pay all your taxes this year.

Then you're free! Up the IRS's tush!
Start a budget, but pop open a beer!
Better yet, you'll probably push
To move Tax Free Day up next year.

Washington will have to budget for real.
Accountability will be required.
If they can't keep their end of the deal
They will all be fired!

UNLIMITED EXPRESS CARD

Before there were credit cards, as such,
All the Rulers, every Dictator,
Had budgets, could only spend so much.
Then came 'Buy Now, Pay Later'.

The scheme would finance more war
And between wars, political fun stuff.
They could balance their budgets and more,
If they put off repayments enough!

It's the 'Unlimited Express'.
Limit, one card per nation.
Pre-approved and credit-checked, no less.
With no 'debit' notification.

So now we're all in the clover!
The Treasurers just back-and-fill.
They keep rolling the balance over
So we never have to pay the bill!

But it grows, it doesn't disappear.
We ignore it, but you can bet
Creditors collect interest each year
On our humungous National Debt.

It hit $30 Trillion recently,
And inflation is starting to foam.
If rates start rising indecently –
Let's just say, "Don't try this at home".

INFLATION

Have you looked in your wallet today?
Perhaps a quick, nervous peek?
And you noticed with growing dismay
It won't last til the end of the week?

Everything's *Up!* Up yours too, government!
You let our standard of living slide!
Our only entertainment
Will be hanging on for the ride.

It's called *inflation*, and it's a shame
For paycheck workers, pensioners too.
But no matter who else they blame,
Washington is doing this to you!

Don't forget the Federal Reserve.
This is what they're *paid* to prevent!
But they've forgotten who they serve
Just like Congress and the President.

They've been spending like drunken sailors!
Wait a minute, that's not funny.
Most days, sailors are teetotalers,
And they're spending their own money.

Let's line up those VIP's
For that sailor, when he's on a toot.
He's got guns and the expertise
To give 'em a 21-gun salute!

KITTY STEALING JEWELRY

(To this caper I do attest:
It is certified public knowledge.
The detective who made the arrest
Posted this on my fridge.)

So where are you off to, Burglar Cat?
To pawn my nice jewels for money?
You rat!
And then whoop it up in Paris and Rome?
And never get caught?
'Cause you'll never come home?
And never stand trial?
Just party and howl?
Ha!
You won't get one mile and your tummy will growl!
I'll tear open a sack and we'll hear your "Meee-owww",
And you'll give it all back
For some cheap kitty chow.

DIGITAL WASTE

Who knew, looking back to the Beginning
When there was just primordial soup,
Before humans even were sinning,
That we were doomed to have digital poop?

I don't know what else to call it.
We flush it from our devices.
You might say, "delete" or, 'uninstall it",
But the word 'poop' really suffices.

Just like your bathroom biffy
Drains to a sewer below,
Your deletion key is a privy.
Well, the waste needs somewhere to go.

Your digital nutrients may fill
Some new primordial sea
If the data you're trying to kill
Turns out to be digital pee.

But if the cyber sewer overflows,
Glop will rise up through cyber plumbing
To your devices! So stay on your toes.
You're gonna hear it coming!

Just don't hit 'delete' like a fool.
That's like flushing a plugged-up stool.
It'll overflow through your computer.
What you need is a roto-rooter!

THE CATAMOUNT

When legends speak of the *Catamount*
In its high-country habitat
They don't mean the 'Cat of the Mountains',
But the *mountain that's really a cat.*

They're supposed to be geological
But mountains can awaken and change.
Catamountains turn biological
In every mountain range.

Their features are simply enormous.
Sheer cliffs might only be cheeks.
While the tails and tall, craggy backbones
Form the actual mountain peaks.

They hibernate under the snowcap.
They're probably sleeping right now.
But next spring they'll wake up hungry,
And *you'll* look like catamount chow!

KOMODOS

Ignoring the gross nitty-gritties,
The job Komodo lizards worked at
Did balance ecological pretties,
But they felt more fearsome than that.

So they added 'Dragon' to their name
Because 'lizard' had a wimpy ring.
It was a dubious claim
And it angered the real Dragon King.

"Bring me a Komodo!" he roared.
But others asked, "Alive – or dead?"
"Alive - if you want the reward!"
"Then do it yourself", they said.

So the Dragon King crossed the sea
And confronted the lizard boss
Who slobbered before Authority,
And seemed totally at a loss.

"I'll call you 'snapdragon' ", laughed the King,
Leaning down very close,
"A flower, a harmless thing!"
Then he got bit on the nose.

Infection burned in him head to toe
His brush with death was dire.
Poor fellow just didn't know
Komodos have their own kind of fire.

GINORMA

The lousy actress, Ginorma,
The largest dragon of all,
Thought she was quite a performer
After drinking enough alcohol.

But her audience always took fright
Even when she wore cute lingerie,
So she searched for a hero or knight
Because champions don't run away.

She even rehearsed what to say
And thought up sweet valentines,
But on stage her mind went astray –
She couldn't remember her lines!

How embarrassing. No one would cheer.
And of course the knight didn't clap.
Ginorma blushed down to her rear,
And then she just ate the poor chap.

THE PONY EXPRESS

The *supply chain*: Solid, easy to make.
Chains are strong. They don't leave a mess.
Except – you guessed it – links do break.
Just ask the Pony Express.

It was their destiny to haul mail,
To gallop across the Wild West.
For America they broke that trail
Because our destiny was manifest!

But nobody told the Paiutes.
To them, honkies were outsiders.
So opening up new supply routes
Was deadly for the riders.

While trying to avoid war parties
More than one rider chewed his last chaw.
One lucky lad survived a tight squeeze
With just an arrow through his jaw.

The Express advertised for orphan lads.
Some say they began to require them.
Lawyers must have hated those ads.
For claims, there'd be no one to hire them.

Supply chains run on diesel now.
No more ponies, like back in the day.
And diesel is *pricey.* Holy cow!
But no worse than good oats and hay.

THE SCARLET DRAGON

Great Spirit gave dragons the fire
In the primary colors of light
To awaken the stars we admire.
So the dragons lit up the night.

It got wild. Seven great firedrakes
With a spectrum of awesome-hot flames
Setting off cosmic fires and earthquakes,
And none of them even had names.

I'd call this one *Red*, wouldn't you?
For his blushing cheeks and his nose?
And the cheeks on his rumble seat too,
Because dragons don't wear any clothes.

CAMELOT

The English, for simply eons
Were not ruled by humans alone.
Dragons bossed all Europeans
Til Arthur pulled that sword out of stone.

Right away like a young fool
He proposed a duel to the death
With the Dragon King, Slobb the Cruel.
Just sword against fiery breath.

The duel would be binding – no excuses!
Both races must agree to the rules!
Dragons leave England if Slobb loses,
If he wins they get the Crown Jewels!

Whew! Was this getting out of control?
Lordy, what if it should go bad?
But Arthur had an ace in the hole.
Old Merlin put a charm on the lad.

Slobb's fire burned his own nose.
That stung, as did the tip of the sword.
The sword paused – in mercy, I suppose
And the dragons fled west, in accord.

So who discovered America?
Columbus already lost out.
The Norskies beat him, you betcha!
But now their claim, too, is in doubt.

EVOLUTION

The theory of evolution
Where fish crawled out of the sea
Became a human attribution
Because Darwin said it should be.

He saw how remote island birds
Changed over centuries
So that proved in a few simple words
That we were once fish if you please.

Too far out? Then try salamanders.
They have legs to crawl out of the sea.
But lacking video from bystanders
We're not sure what relation they'd be.

Maybe the first one was real pretty
Yet stern and tough as a bearcat.
Raised twelve mud puppies and a kitty.
Who wouldn't love a grandma like that?

But what if the human condition
Slips a cog? Starts to get worse?
Is evolution like a transmission?
Could it get jammed in reverse?

Humanity needs a babysitter
If Twitter is any barometer!
Anyone who tweets on Twitter
Should submit to a rectal thermometer.

DRAGON TREASURE HOARDS

The Great Spirit used seven
    firedrakes
To light up Heaven's void
With the beauty that cosmic fire
    makes.
Nice job! But now they're
    unemployed.

We've heard about 'idle hands'.
It's the same with idle claws.
It holds true across all lands.
They find mischief *just because.*

The dragons turned their attention
To building treasure hoards,
Laughing off, I should mention,
The disapproval of the Lord.

Earth had just what they were
    looking for.
Oh, the serfs were 'chewy', we've
    been told,
But there were *Monarchies* galore,
And the rulers all had gold!

The dragons plundered it all
Opposed only by doggy barks.
Knights-in-armor were far too small
To fight the dragon patriarchs.

With their treasuries looted and
    burned
What could Royals do? Spend less?
It don't work that way, we have
    learned.
They just sent out the IRS.

Great Spirit intervened that day.
The Royal treasuries were restored.
Dragons were sent light years away.
And the IRS was ignored.

Dragons did return, a younger race
As soon as they were able.
Gold draws a crowd! But now they
    would face
The Knights of the Round Table.

Thus serfs bested both boss and
    beast!
Just once, thanks to the Great Spirit.
That was fun, but they still get
    fleeced
By the IRS, the way I hear it.

REYNARD

Behold the fox.
So clever and quick.
Lord of the field and briar.

So clever, so quick
He can't be caught
By rain, or wind, or fire.

Nor the vixen,
Even quicker,
And often a witch in disguise.

A witch by night
On a living broomstick
Flying through moonlit skies.

They're the craftiest critters on 4 legs,
No 'ifs' or 'ands' or 'buts'.
Yet there are days (a lot of days)
When the pixies drive them nuts.

GOBLIN-VAX

Lockdowns and testing and scares – oh my!
It's the wicked witch covid virus!
We must take the wizard vax – or die!
Goblins found it very desirous.

Urpgob, their Boss, the great thinker
Quickly connected the dots
And being a heavy drinker,
He liked the sound of "free shots".

Goblins in hazardous waste jobs
Collected expired batches.
Half was supposed to be Urpgob's,
But most went right down their hatches.

They snorted serum for a high,
Which left some of them frowning.
You never know until you try -
But the side effect was drowning.

Some got hooked on boosters too,
And there's a fix for that abuse:
They set up a booster shot *drive*-through!
And did so well they made the news.

They put on scrubs and advertised.
Business boomed and they did lots.
But drivers were always surprised
That nurses gave themselves the shots.

FIREBALL

Some dragons set forests a-blazing.
A few can make whole cities sweat.
Their fire is simply amazing.
But this is the hottest one yet!

He scorches two people for breakfast,
And broils another for brunch.
Then he checks his crystal ball menu
To see who he's roasting for lunch.

Is it alien, that fiery breath?
Where on earth does the fire come from?
He's drug-free, so it's not crack or meth.
And we dare not ask his sweet mum.

It's probably nuclear fission
That powers the flaming giants.
That's the scientific suspicion.
But they don't leave their bodies to science.

Anyhow, what does it matter
If he's humanoid or alien?
Because even if it's the latter
His appetite is mammalian.

THE DRAGON CIVIL WAR

Dragons would not have been known
Outside their home Constellation,
But just half – and that half *alone,*
Policed all their conversation.

You just know it couldn't stay that way.
Dragons hate being told what to do.
Even worse, being told what to *say.*
So violence festered and grew.

A dragon civil war caught fire
That was brewing for many years.
The censored ones vented their ire
And burned off their enemy's ears.

That's when the war took a pause.
Not that war is something they're bad at –
The Elites just shut up because
They couldn't hear what to be mad at.

Since scolds like that never quit,
And lucky for the Milky Way,
The others took their Free Speech and split,
And it's found everywhere today!

www.ingramcontent.com/pod-product-compliance
Lightning Source LLC
Chambersburg PA
CBHW081328090726
47907CB00010B/2409